SAVED BY THE ALIEN WARRIOR

HOPE HART

CHAPTER ONE

B eth

FOUR WEEKS EARLIER

"I NEED A BREAK."

I turn and wince as my eyes meet Charlie's. While none of us are looking our best after being abducted, crash-landing on this planet, and being forced to walk for hours, Charlie looks like she's half dead.

Blood covers her face, and she's so pale that she looks like a ghost.

Karok frowns, and I eye him. After the crash, all of us human women were trapped in a cage on the ship. The Voildi showed up and killed the surviving purple aliens who'd bought us after we'd been abducted from Earth by the Grivath and sold on a slave planet.

Karok seems to be the leader of this group.

From the look on Ellie's face, I'm not the only one who finds this rescue a little too convenient. The Voildi are a pale-yellow color, and they're almost naked except for the thin, dirty loincloths they're wearing. A few of them are carrying long spears, and one of them keeps turning his head, scanning the area warily.

"We must keep moving if we are to make it to our camp by nightfall."

Nevada shifts, her eyes narrowing as she examines the Voildi. From the expression on her face, it's clear that she's not impressed by what she sees.

"Charlie isn't feeling well," she says. "We can take ten minutes."

We all stop, and I move closer to the edge of the clearing as a few of the other women huddle around Charlie. Most of us were in our pajamas when we were taken, and we've used some of the material as bandages and slings. Charlie's wound has bled through the makeshift bandage though, and I lean closer to Ivy.

"I'm worried about her," I murmur.

Ivy nods. "She has a concussion," she says. "Her pupils are dilated, and she's been puking into bushes along the way. She needs to rest." Ivy's dark eyes scan the group. "We all do."

None of us are looking good. Truthfully, we're lucky that we all survived the crash.

Ivy shifts on her feet, wincing. "Wish I was wearing shoes when I was kidnapped," she mutters. She glances at my feet and raises her eyebrows. I curl my toes, embarrassed.

"I'm a dancer," I say. After hours of walking barefoot on sharp stones and sticks, most of us are cut and bleeding. But my feet are covered in older bruises, two of my toenails are black, and one of my cracked toes is still covered in a dirty bandage.

She nods, and Ellie steps forward.

"Please," she addresses Karok. "Do you know where we can find some water?"

Ivy tenses beside me, and I glance at her, but she's staring at Karok, who has a weird smile on his face.

He shakes his head, and Ellie scowls.

The thought of water makes my hands shake I want it so badly. My tongue keeps sticking to the roof of my mouth, and I have the kind of headache that only comes from dehydration.

"Oh my God!" Zoey screams. I turn, stumbling back as three giant men suddenly jump out of the bushes where they must have been hiding. They're roaring as they attack the Voildi, and my mouth drops open as I take them in.

Ivy reaches out and pulls Zoey toward us as we move further back. The men are huge—likely at least seven feet tall. One of them has ripped his shirt, and his shoulder and chest make it evident that while the men are certainly male, they could never be mistaken for humans.

Scales, I think distantly as I stare at the blue-green pattern on his skin. *I'm pretty sure those are scales.*

All of them have longer hair than I'm used to seeing on Earth, and more importantly, they're all carrying huge swords. The Voildi let out high-pitched growls, immediately surrounding them.

One of the huge men laughs, baring his teeth as the Voildi draw their own swords.

Karok's head hits the ground.

It happens so quickly that I almost miss it, one of the huge men slashing his sword lightning fast.

I lean over and puke, my eyes watering as I gag on what

little is left in my stomach. I lift my head, and a scream rips from my throat as a hard arm encircles my waist and pulls me back.

I throw elbows, but someone's lifting me. The arm is yellow. Yellow like the Voildi who were just taking us to safety. The arm is clamped around my waist like a vise, and no matter how desperately I claw at it, it's not budging.

Are these Voildi rescuing us from the fight? If so, why didn't they help the other women too?

When I was younger, I had panic attacks. I would be walking to dance class or on the bus, and suddenly I'd be certain I was going to die—right then, in that moment.

Doctors call it a feeling of impending doom. All I know is that there was nothing worse than suddenly feeling that something was very, very wrong.

This is that same feeling. I know with complete certainty that something terrible is going to happen. And I sure as hell shouldn't be separated from the other women.

"Help!" I scream, lifting my head. I catch a flash of Ivy's red hair out the corner of my eye. How many of us have been taken?

No one's coming to help, and the fighting continues. I choke out a sob, struggling uselessly as thin tree branches hit my face.

I pound my hands against the Voildi's back, but it's as if I'm a bug. Blood pounds in my head as he begins running.

I scream again, and this time, the Voildi makes a sound of displeasure. Ivy's yell reaches my ears, and another woman is shrieking like a wailing cat as we're carried through the forest.

Splashes sound, and I raise my head slightly. We're walking through water. It's torture to see water so close as we cross the small stream, and I'd do anything to be able to reach down and grab a handful.

The alien takes large strides, and I realize we're going up a hill. We reach the top, and I groan as I'm unceremoniously dumped on the ground.

"Ow, fuck!" I glare up at my captor and freeze.

He's a Voildi. His skin is the same shade of yellow as the others', his teeth sharp and pointed as he bares them at me. I glance around as a scuffle sounds, and Ivy elbows one of the Voildi in the face. Unfortunately, he's fucking fast. His hand lashes out and slaps her hard enough that she drops to her knees, cursing as she stumbles back up to her feet.

Zoey is dumped next to me, and we both watch as Ivy dances back from the Voildi.

I blink as I stare at him.

These Voildi are dressed differently than the others, and they're wearing actual clothes, without a loincloth to be seen.

My eyes widen as I hear a roar in the distance. We're still close to the other women. And these assholes aren't our rescuers at all.

I meet Zoey's eyes, and both of us open our mouths, screaming. If the others can hear us, maybe they'll be able to—

A Voildi grabs me by the hair, pulling me to my feet and slapping his hand over my mouth. Zoey trembles next to me, while Ivy takes another slap to the face, and the Voildi she's fighting pulls out a cloth, gagging her with quick movements.

Her eyes meet mine, and I almost flinch at the rage in them. I struggle, but I'm hopelessly outweighed.

The Voildi may not be oversized and muscled like the

massive sword-waving aliens who attacked, but they're strong and still larger than us.

One of them mutters something to the others, and they hold us still for long moments. Ivy is doing something with her hands, and my eyes widen. I glance away, checking that none of the Voildi are watching.

She's ripping her pajamas. They're bright pink, with Mickey Mouse printed on them. I blow out a breath. Thank God Ivy is with us. While I'm freaking out, she clearly has some kind of plan in mind.

She crumples up a small piece of material in her fist, and then we wait.

The Voildi tense as voices sound, and I struggle wildly as a low one reaches us. Whoever those giant alien warriors are, the other women have obviously decided to trust them. And since they're not the ones holding us here against our will, I'm more than ready to trust them too.

Tears prick my eyes as the voices fade. The other Voildi relax, and then Zoey and I are gagged too before we're all thrown over their shoulders again.

I reach for my gag, and the Voildi behind us slaps my hand away.

"Take it off, and we will tie your hands," he says.

The Voildi carrying me seems to take the lead, and we travel for hours.

I try to keep track of where we're going, but every time I lift my head, all I see is the Voildi carrying Zoey. He likes to smirk at me, and I memorize his face. When I get free...

I snort. Yeah, that's real likely.

I've always been a big believer in karma. We live in an unfair world, and when someone chooses to be a dick, sometimes the only thought you have to cling to is that one day, karma will rise up and slap them across the face.

What goes around comes around.

So how and why did this happen to me? I keep to myself. I've never murdered anyone. Sure, I tell a few white lies, but I don't cheat or steal. I'm a good person, goddamnit.

I've worked hard my whole life to achieve what has just been ripped away from me.

Whatever I did in a past life must've been a real doozy. 'Cause that bitch karma has just hit me real hard.

Zarix

"You've only been at camp for three days. If you want to leave already, why don't you join Varish's hunting party?"

I scowl at Dexar, who raises his eyebrow as he sits languidly on his throne.

"You know I prefer to hunt alone."

"The others are talking. 'Why does Zarix get to hunt alone?' they ask." He's obviously mimicking one of his advisers. "'Why won't he take a mate?'"

I feel my frown deepen. "You are the qatai. Who are they to question you?"

Dexar smiles, but I'm not stupid enough to believe he will be content with the stroke to his ego. Dexar may be the tribe king now, but he was once a hunter himself. And his strategies in battle and defense have ensured that our tribe is the largest of all the Braxians'.

We own more land and wealth than all the other tribes combined. Our warriors are well fed, and while we suffer just as other tribes suffer from the shortage of females, we have only one true enemy.

The Voildi.

My blood heats, and I fight to keep my rage from showing on my face. If Dexar believes that I am on the edge, he will refuse to allow this mission.

"They're making plans," I tell him, forcing my voice to remain even. "I believe they are planning to attack a Braxian tribe."

All amusement disappears from Dexar's face. "What makes you believe this?"

"My sources say that some of the Voildi packs have been seen meeting in private. They have never done this before."

Voildi hunt in small numbers, taking food back to their packs, which are usually made up of fewer than fifty of the creatures. For this reason, they have never been a true threat to Braxian tribes. Even the smallest tribe would have enough warriors to fight off an attack from a Voildi pack—likely without taking any casualties themselves.

But if the Voildi are cooperating...

My hands fist, and I take a deep breath as I force them to relax.

Dexar examines me with cool eyes. "You believe they are working together?" he asks.

I nod. "I think the small thefts and scuffles have been nothing more than diversions as they take note of our defenses and examine how each tribe operates."

He stands and waves away a servant who offers him a plate of food. Dexar jerks his head, and we move through the crowd and out of the huge kradi where he holds court.

We enter the meeting room, and Dexar gestures for me to sit as he takes a seat himself.

In spite of the seriousness of our conversation, I feel a jolt of amusement. Dexar lounges in this chair as if it, too, is a throne. If I asked his mother, I would bet that she would tell me that he came out of the womb with an imperious, slightly bored expression on his face and let out a heavy sigh as he took in all the fuss.

"Rakiz has told me that they, too, are seeing an increase in Voildi attacks," he says. "One of them managed to steal a mishua from their pen."

I raise an eyebrow. Rakiz's tribe is one of the largest, and his warriors are to be feared. If the Voildi have dared to steal from them...

"They're getting braver," I say.

Dexar nods, his eyes on me. "If it is as you believe and they're working together, we must know which tribe they're planning to attack."

Triumph hits me, and I fight to keep it from showing. Dexar is well aware of my need to make the Voildi pay, but if he believes I am unable to focus on the task, he will send someone else in my place.

"This will require stealth," I tell him. "Which is why I need to go alone."

He gives me a long look, and I meet his eyes without looking away. Finally, he nods.

"Find out everything you can about how many Voildi are working together and the tribe they're targeting. Once we know, we can prepare the tribe and lay a trap."

I bare my teeth in what I'm sure is a feral smile. "And finally take care of the Voildi for good."

CHAPTER TWO

B^{eth}

I GROAN AS I HIT THE GROUND AGAIN. MY MOUTH IS SO DRY that if I wasn't gagged, I'd be begging our captors for water.

We're in another clearing—this one much smaller than the last. I pull my legs close and watch as Ivy and Zoey each fall to the ground with a thump.

Zoey turns sheet white, and I wince for her. We were taken by the Grivath to a slave planet and sold. Zoey tripped and fell when we were being loaded onto the ship by our new "owners," and one of them kicked her in the ribs. Hard.

She looks out of it, her face gray and her forehead covered in sweat. Ivy pulls herself up until she's sitting on a fallen tree, and we watch as the Voildi huddle, ignoring us as they talk amongst themselves.

The Voildi have been careful to erase their tracks— going as far as to head in one direction and then walk back- ward before switching to another direction. They must be pretty scared of the huge warriors if they're making such an effort.

Ivy shifts, and I almost grin as she stuffs another piece of material inside the log. Her pajamas are nothing but rags now, but if anyone comes looking for us, maybe they'll be able to spot the clues she's left behind.

I put my hands behind me and begin ripping up grass as one of the Voildi rolls his shoulders.

"Let's switch," he says loudly, glancing at me. "I'll carry the skinny one."

I frown at him, and my hand comes up almost of its own volition as I wag my middle finger at him.

Ivy laughs around her gag, and even Zoey winks at me. The Voildi examines me for a long moment before finally turning away dismissively.

Good to know these guys are struggling. They're not much taller than Ivy, and while they're fast on their feet, it takes serious muscle to pick up a human and carry them for hours.

The Voildi lift us again, and I slump, letting myself become deadweight. We're not going to be able to escape anytime soon, so I may as well make it as difficult for them to carry me as possible.

I glance up at the sky, watching as the green darkens. It'll be night soon, and our chances of freedom decrease as we get further from the others. I grind my teeth as the Voildi murmur about what to do with us.

"Not much flesh," the one carrying me says, pinching the back of my thigh. I wiggle, trying fruitlessly to knee him, and he laughs.

"More bone than anything else," his friend agrees from behind us. "This one looks juicy." He slaps his hand against Zoey's ass, and I gag.

Are they talking about...eating us?

"You know what Killis said. Bring them back alive. He has plans."

Zoey is silent, and I crane my head, but all I can see are her legs. She must be in excruciating pain upside down. I'm sure she has at least one cracked rib after the kick she took from that purple motherfucker on the slave planet.

When we walked off the crashed ship, I saw him slumped over, dead next to the stairs.

See? Karma.

Finally, their steps slow, and I flinch at the sound of laughing.

"I knew you'd find them. All we had to do was follow Atar's pack. Where are the rest?"

The Voildi carrying me growls. "Braxians," he says, and his friend curses.

Once again, my ass hits the ground, and I survey our surroundings.

We're in a large clearing, staring at a cave entrance, and all eyes are on us. There must be twenty or thirty Voildi here, and more are coming out of the cave.

"Get up," one of them says, and I slowly get to my feet. Zoey's face is bloodless as she makes it to her knees, and one of the Voildi steps forward, raising his hand as if to hit her.

Ivy jumps in front of Zoey, eyes wild, and I help Zoey to her feet. She flicks a glance at me and nods, and we watch as one of the Voildi reaches out to casually backhand Ivy.

She's faster this time, smoothly ducking under his arm and punching him in the face. His friends burst out laughing, and he reddens as he cups his nose.

If my mouth wasn't married to my gag, I'd smile.

He steps forward, and Ivy raises her fists. I wince. We're

hopelessly outnumbered and guaranteed to lose a brawl with these assholes.

"Jasit," a voice says, warning clear in the tone, and all the Voildi turn. This is obviously their leader, and I glare at him as he examines us with dead eyes.

"Where are the rest?" he asks.

"The Braxians showed up," the Voildi who carried Ivy says. "They killed the hunters from Atar's pack."

The Voildi nods, still examining us.

"Are you sure we can't eat them?" Jasit asks, and Dead Eyes smiles.

"I have plans for them," he says. "Meat can be found anywhere on this planet. But females are a precious commodity."

I feel like I should be celebrating the fact that I'm not going to be eaten, but I'm too tired. And truthfully, anyone who would buy people from the Voildi is probably going to make us wish we were dead anyway.

Dead Eyes glances back at us and gestures to the cave entrance. "Walk."

Ivy has obviously gotten ahold of herself because she leads the way, and we sandwich Zoey between us. No part of me wants to walk into this cave, but if we're going to escape, we need to wait for the right moment.

We're in a dimly lit passageway, although there are a few torches flickering in place against the rocky walls. I stumble over something—either a bone or a white rock—and barely prevent myself from slamming into Zoey's back. The passageway smells like rot and decay, and I can also scent some sort of meat cooking.

While I'm ravenous, the smell turns my stomach after the recent discussions about our edibility.

After a couple of minutes, the passage opens up further,

and we no longer need to walk single file. Then it opens into a large space, where more Voildi are huddled around a fire. My eyes widen as I take in a group of female Voildi, a few of them holding children to their breasts.

Somehow I imagined that these monsters sprang from the ground fully formed. I turn as Dead Eyes steps into the cave, and then I'm cursing as one of the Voildi unties my gag and rips it from my mouth.

Dead Eyes gestures to a Voildi who's missing an ear, and he offers me a waterskin.

My throat and mouth are like the desert, but I hesitate, and Dead Eyes gives me another chilling smile.

"We want you alive," he says, still smiling. "So drink, or we will pour it down your throat."

I drink.

The water tastes nasty, but it's all we've got. I turn to see if I need to save some for Ivy and Zoey, but they're gulping down water as well. I guzzle until it's all gone, then grimace as I realize I've probably drunk it too fast.

Dead Eyes points to a corner, far from the fire, and we move toward the thin furs. Obviously this is where we're bedding down for the night. And now that we're surrounded by so many Voildi, we won't be escaping.

I meet Ivy's eyes, and she nods, reading my mind. We sit down with our backs against the wall, and one of the women hands us each a plate. I poke at the food, still nauseated at the discovery that we've been taken by cannibals, but Ivy bravely tastes it first.

"It's fish," she murmurs, and I shove a bite in my mouth, desperate for food.

It's surprisingly tender and tastes fresh, and I finish my plate within a few moments. The Voildi mostly ignore us as they bed down, but my heart sinks as I realize they're all sleeping in the same area.

Ivy leans her head back against the wall and gestures for us to do the same.

"We're not getting out of here tonight," she says. "But that's okay. We're not in good condition, and we need sleep anyway."

I nod. "If they've got plans, they might move us."

"Or they could bring those plans to us," Zoey murmurs.

Ivy shakes her head. "This looks temporary. Look, those guys are arguing over blankets, and it's clear that this camp has been hastily set up."

"So what do we do?"

Ivy sighs, and I glance at her as her mouth twists.

"I was a dumbass and showed them I could fight. Now they're going to watch me more closely. They know Zoey's injured, and they've already discounted you as a thin weakling," she says, rolling her eyes at me.

In spite of the situation, I almost grin. Ballet dancers? We're tough. We put our bodies through hell. I've taped broken toes together and danced en pointe. I've rehearsed all day, six days a week, for years. I've torn ligaments and danced through a stress fracture.

Thin? Sure. A weakling? Nope.

Ivy clamps her mouth shut for a moment when one of the Voildi comes close. Then she lowers her voice even further, barely moving her lips.

"We need to be realistic. We're outnumbered. By a lot. Chances are, we're not all making it out of here together."

Zoey lets out a choked sob, and I reach over and grab her hand.

"We can't split up," I say.

Ivy narrows her eyes at me. "We do whatever is best for

all of us. If even one of us can get away, we can get help for the others."

I glance away, unconvinced. I really need to put on my big girl panties, but I'm not sure which thought is worse—leaving the other two women behind or being left behind myself.

The rest of the night is quiet. Eventually most of the Voildi fall asleep, but there are guards left near the entrance, and I'm sure they're also posted outside. We take turns staying awake to keep an eye out for threats and any chances to escape. When it's my turn to rest, I sleep like the dead until Zoey shakes my shoulder, and I jolt awake.

It wasn't a nightmare. We're still here on a strange planet after we were abducted from our beds.

When the Arcav invaded, all the females on Earth had to give blood samples to see if we were compatible to be mates. We lost four women from our dance company, and I heaved a sigh of relief when I wasn't a match.

All the work I put in—the thousands of hours of rehearsals, the injuries, the sacrifices—it was worth it. I kept dancing even when the world seemed to fall apart and people fled the cities in droves. When they gradually returned, I was ready.

I made it. After years of toil in the corps, I was a principal dancer. In fact, I was about to dance the role of Odette in *Swan Lake* for the fifth time. Those thirty-two fouetté turns were *mine*.

And it was all stolen from me.

"Beth, are you awake?" Zoey's voice is a hoarse whisper.

"Yeah. How are you feeling?"

Zoey doesn't look much better than she did earlier. Her face has a little more color, but she's sitting hunched over as if she's protecting her side. "I'm okay."

We're silent as we watch the Voildi. It seems as if Ivy was right and this cave is just a pit stop. I'm already jumping out of my skin, itching with the need to feel fresh air on my face.

A Voildi approaches and hands us a waterskin to share but no food. A few minutes later, another one walks past, and I can't resist. I thrust out my leg, and he trips over my ankle, falling to his knees.

All three of us snigger as he face-plants, his forehead hitting the dirt floor of the cave with a dull thump.

"Whoops," I say as he makes it to his feet, turning on me with bared teeth. "My bad."

Dead Eyes appears, and everyone goes silent. While the smile is no longer lingering around his mouth, the look on his face is just as scary.

"We may want you alive, but that doesn't mean you need to be healthy," he says softly.

"It was an accident," I say sweetly even as I shiver at his tone. "I needed to stretch."

He stares at me for a moment longer and then gestures to another one of his men. The Voildi orders us to our feet, and we file out of the cave with the rest of the group.

It's a clear day, and while it's chilly, I take a moment to appreciate the sun on my skin.

"I need the bathroom," Ivy announces loudly, and the Voildi closest to us look at each other in confusion.

She sighs. "I need to piss." She crosses her legs and bounces in place for a moment, and they finally seem to get it, one of them snorting.

"Killis?" he asks, and Dead Eyes approaches. At least I know his name now. And I'm not at all surprised that it has the word *kill* in it.

The shorter Voildi turns to him, muttering a few words.

Killis doesn't look pleased, but he points to three Voildi, who lead Ivy into the forest.

Three Voildi for one human. Seems like overkill, but Ivy has already proven that she's not to be messed with. They're back a few moments later, and Ivy meets my eyes with a slight shake of her head.

Shit.

We're surrounded by Voildi as we start walking. I focus on putting one foot in front of the other, and we've been trudging through the forest for at least a few hours when Ivy tilts her head at me.

"I can't," I mutter.

"You have to. You're our only hope."

If I'm our only hope, we're all screwed.

I glance at Zoey. She's not doing well at all. One of the Voildi is carrying her after she collapsed, unable to walk any further.

I wait until the Voildi close to us start talking about a tribe they're planning to invade. I hope the tribe manages to kill them all.

"I'm not really the hero type," I mutter. "I'm more decorative."

Ivy grins at me, and then her face hardens. "Buck up, champ. You're on."

I sigh, sway dizzily, and drop to my knees.

"Get up," one of the Voildi orders, swinging his leg back. I get to my feet, stumbling. The last thing I want is to be injured the way Zoey is.

I trip over a branch and hit the ground again, and one of the Voildi picks me up, throwing me over his shoulder with a curse.

Excellent.

We travel like this for what must be close to an hour while I summon my courage. And then I squirm.

"I need to pee," I say, my voice weak.

The Voildi lets out a low growl but mutters to his friends, "We will catch up."

Fear hits me like a truck, and as he turns, I raise my head, catching one last glimpse of Zoey's pale face and Ivy's bloodless lips as she gives me a nod.

I've only got one shot at this. Fail, and we're all screwed. Oh, and they may just decide I'm more trouble than I'm worth and eat me after all.

Once again, I'm dumped on my ass as the Voildi steps behind a tree.

The others move away, and I take my time fumbling with the thin cord of my pajama shorts, pretending as if it's difficult to untie.

"Hurry up," the Voildi says.

"I can't go with you watching." My voice trembles, and my hands shake.

He narrows his eyes at me, glances around, and then looks me up and down. I hunch my shoulders, glancing away.

I'm just a weak, skinny female. I'm not a threat to you.

Finally, after a long, fraught moment, he turns his back.

My eyes dart, but I don't have time to be picky as I reach for a large branch. This will have to do.

I take three big steps and swing the branch like my life depends on it.

Because it does.

CHAPTER THREE

B eth

CRACK.

The first blow stuns the Voildi, who falls to his knees, disorientated. He opens his mouth to call out, and I slam the branch into his face again.

Blood flies, and I dart back as he attempts to get to his knees, reaching for me.

I hit him again and again until finally he's either unconscious or dead, and I'm panting, bile rising.

I wipe my hand over my face, gagging when it comes away red from blood splatter.

We've been too long. The other Voildi are going to come looking for him at any moment.

I whirl. We came from that gap between the trees, which means I need to go in the opposite direction.

I drop the branch, tuck my chin close to my chest, and run like hell.

Branches and rocks cut my feet, but I block out the pain, focusing on putting as much distance as I can between myself and the Voildi. I scan my surroundings, mentally discarding hiding places. They'll find me for sure. I'm making too much noise as I crash through the forest, the long, finger-like branches of the trees whipping me in the face as I run. But it can't be helped.

Roars sound from behind me, and I pick up the pace, leaping over a fallen tree. The Voildi are fast, and they'll be on me within minutes if I can't find somewhere to hide.

Up a tree?

I glance up, panting, my breath almost a sob. These trees are like none I've ever seen before. Other than the occasional long, sweeping branch hanging down onto the forest floor, the white tree trunks are as smooth as concrete. The Voildi will see me for sure.

I jump another log, crying out at the pain in my foot as I step on something sharp. And then I freeze.

What's that noise?

I attempt to tune out the sound of the Voildi as they get closer and focus instead on the thundering sound to my right.

Please, God, tell me that's a waterfall.

I sprint toward the sound, darting through trees until I see it.

It's about thirty feet high, the water crashing into a pool that flows into a wide river. I glance over my shoulder as the voices get closer, and I tremble as I switch my attention back to the waterfall.

If I jump, I could hit a rock. The water might not be deep enough, and my body could go splat like a pancake. I could get trapped against a rock, and if the water is too cold, hypothermia is a real possibility.

But I'm our only chance.

"You!"

The Voildi make my choice for me, and I back up a couple of steps, take a deep breath, and leap from the cliff, aiming away from the rocks.

I almost scream as the water rushes toward me, but then I'm under, thankfully still alive. I gasp in reflex, inhaling cold water as it engulfs me. Terror shoots through my body as I fight my way to the surface, and then I break free, coughing and spluttering as I clear my lungs.

I don't have time to celebrate. If the Voildi follow me, I'm dead. I don't look up. I take another deep breath, ignoring the urge to cough, and dunk underwater, swimming toward the slight drop into the river below.

I wince as my knees scrape rocks, and then I'm over and in the river, coughing water from my lungs as I'm swept away.

My feet brush the ground in a few places, and I could probably stand, but I let the water carry me far from the Voildi. Unless they jump in, they won't be able to catch up now.

I try not to think about any alien animals that could be making this river their home. If I do, the urge to swim to the shore is almost overwhelming, and I need to get further away.

A bird calls above my head, and then there's nothing but the roar of the water as I pull my knees to my chest and let the river take me far away.

It's cold. Cold enough that I probably don't have long before hypothermia sets in. I'll need to get onto land soon and dry off. The sun is out, hidden behind clouds in the turquoise sky. If I can dry off before it gets dark, I'll be okay.

When I was a kid, Dad took me camping. After I was

born, Mom couldn't have any more kids, so I was somewhat of a tomboy when I wasn't dancing.

"Respect the wild," he'd say, "or face the consequences."

I'm shivering uncontrollably, so I begin looking for an exit point. The river is now shallow enough that I can stand, so I wade toward the bank. Pretty purple wildflowers are growing along the side of the river, next to bright-pink mushrooms that I avoid as I haul myself out of the water. With my luck, they're probably poisonous.

My shivering increases as the air hits my wet skin, and my stomach howls. I'm starving.

I look around, searching for some kind of path or even a sign to show me which way to go. But there's nothing. For one long moment, loneliness crashes through me, hitting me like a truck. I can't give in to it. If I let myself brood, I'll curl up by the wildflowers and never get up.

The trees are different in this part of the forest. While the other trees were white, with long, thin branches, these are more similar to the trees found on Earth. But the branches are so thick, with so many leaves, that they're currently blocking out the sun.

My teeth are chattering as I trudge through the forest, moving away from the river. I have no real plan except to find someone, anyone, who can help me rescue Ivy and Zoey and locate the other human women.

The bugs find me delicious, and I'm constantly slapping them away as I pick up the pace. I have to get to some form of civilization before dark, or I'm in big trouble.

Time passes. I don't know how much time, but my mouth is once again dry, and my hands are shaking. My steps are getting smaller and closer together, and my feet are bloody and bruised as I stumble over sticks and rocks.

Eventually I see signs of civilization. Not a town or

anything. That would be too easy. But I find a trail and almost drop to my knees in relief. If I just follow the trail, maybe it'll lead me to someone. Anyone.

I pick up my speed, hope driving me forward.

SLAM.

I scream. My body goes one way while my leg stays in place, and I fall to the ground as my calf is engulfed in agony. The pain is horrific, and I almost black out as I raise my head enough to look down.

My leg is caught in some kind of trap. Likely it's for a wild animal. And I bet the locals know how to avoid this type of trap. It's metal, with sharp spikes that remind me of a bear trap, only much nastier.

I take a deep breath and reach for the claws of the trap, attempting to open them.

I'd have more luck opening a portal back to Earth.

My blood is dripping onto the forest floor, and black dots dance in front of my eyes. My hands shake, and I gag as I realize the metal prongs have dug deep through the skin and muscle of my calf.

Fuck.

Zarix

I'm close to Balix when I smell it. Blood. I keep one hand on my sword as I stalk down the trail. Knowing the Voildi, they have once again trapped someone for tonight's meal.

My hands fist at the thought.

I follow my nose, and a growl leaves my throat. I was right. A girl-child has been caught, her leg pinned in one of the vicious traps the Voildi leave throughout their territory.

She is crumpled on the ground, and I have a moment of despair as I imagine her parents looking for their dead daughter. I frown, and then I'm kneeling by her side as I lean close.

She is breathing.

I examine the trap and wince. The muscle of her calf has been punctured, and her blood runs from her leg in a steady drip.

I grind my teeth. I don't have time to spare taking this child to a healer. But only a monster would leave her. I am not a monster. Yet.

I lean closer and frown. Her clothes are strange, and I feel my eyes widen as I examine her body. She is not Braxian. In fact, she is not of any species I have seen before.

And she is not a child.

My mouth drops open as I take in the small, round breasts beneath the strange shirt that clings to her body like a second skin. This is a tiny, delicate female.

A female who is opening her eyes.

Those eyes are a deep blue, glazed with pain.

"Well," she grinds out, her teeth clenched. "Are you going to help me or what?"

I raise an eyebrow. She speaks a language I have never heard before, and it is only the translator in my ear that allows me to understand her.

"I need to open the trap. This will hurt."

She nods, and something in my chest clenches as her small hands clutch at the dirt of the forest floor and her eyes squeeze shut.

I study the trap and scowl. The mechanism has broken, and I will need to manually pull the metal prongs from her leg.

"I'm sorry, female."

I begin my task, clenching my teeth as I start forcing open the trap. She screams, and I do my best to block out her pained cries as I try to bend the prongs.

After a few moments, she finally passes out, and I curse as I pull her leg free.

It's a mess.

She needs a healer, and I know of only one who will take her with no questions. Unfortunately, she is located in the opposite direction of where I'm going.

Perhaps I could locate a hunting party from our tribe and convince them to take her with them?

The female begins to shiver. Her skin is cool, clammy, and pale, and her breathing comes in fast pants. I growl in frustration, but her condition makes my decision for me. I gently lift her into my arms, stunned at how light she is. I put my fingers to my mouth and whistle, and Rexi—my mishua—appears, leaning down to sniff at the female.

I gently lay the female in the saddle and then pull myself up behind her, taking her in my arms. Then, with one last glance toward Balix, I grit my teeth and turn the mishua toward Honit.

The female wakes once more, and again I have the sense of falling into her gaze.

"Help," she says.

"I am."

"Other...women. Ivy. Zoey."

There are others like her? How did she end up alone and trapped in Voildi territory?

"Where are they, female?"

Her eyes roll back in her head, and she loses consciousness again. A blessing, for sure, given the state of her leg.

Her hair is long and dark, tangled and damp against my

arm as I support her shoulders. She has delicate features, with large eyes and a mouth that seems too big for her face. Those lush lips have a blue tinge, and I urge Rexi into a faster pace.

We are not far from the healer, although I now will not make it to Balix before dark. I scowl down at the inconvenience in my arms, and my heart pounds faster as I take in the slight sweat on her brow.

I'm off the mishua and running toward the healer's small hut when we arrive, and Sonis meets me at the door.

"I need your help."

With her slitted dark gaze, she takes in the female in my arms. "I gathered."

A small blue face peeks out at me from behind his mother's skirts, and I raise one eyebrow.

"Who is this?"

Sonis gestures for me to step inside, and I duck my head as I enter, my eyes adjusting to the dim light.

She leads me toward the room she uses for healing, glancing back at me with amusement. "You remember my son, Javir."

"I remember a boy of six or seven summers. This is a full-grown male."

The boy in question grins at me, revealing gaps in his teeth.

"Have you been fighting again?"

He shakes his head. "Nuh-uh."

"Then what happened to your teeth?"

"They fell out."

I frown at his tone, which suggests that I am not asking smart questions, and then I remember. Unlike my people, whose teeth grow with us as we mature, his race has two sets of teeth.

Sonis is gesturing to the small bed, and I place the female down.

"Where did you find such a female?" she asks.

"In the forest. She had her leg stuck in a Voildi trap."

Sonis's eyes turn haunted, and she whirls away, reaching for the instruments she uses for healing.

The female's eyes crack open once more, cloudy with confusion. "Where am I?"

"You are being healed." I say. "You may want to pass out again. This will not be pleasant."

Sonis elbows me aside and presses a cup to the female's lips. "Drink this. What is your name?"

The female complies, and I wipe away a few drops that escape her lips.

"Beth." Her voice is drowsy, and it doesn't take long before she is unconscious again.

Beth. A simple, beautiful, foreign name. I roll it over my tongue, and then I move away from the strange female as Sonis gets to work.

"She is malnourished," she says, and I run my eyes over the female's body as I lean against the wall.

Her body is thin and fragile, as if she has gone without food for a long time. And yet her muscles are long and lean, toned in a way I have not seen before.

"She's pretty, Mama," Javir says, and I feel the corner of my mouth curl.

Sonis smiles at her son and then gets back to work. Thankfully whatever was in the concoction she gave Beth— I taste her name again—is keeping her unconscious.

"The trap did some damage. This will take time."

I nod. "I will go hunt."

Sonis opens her mouth to protest and then slams it shut,

nodding gratefully, and I take one last look at the strange female before I turn and stalk away.

Beth

I wake, gasping at the roaring pain that travels up my leg, making me writhe.

"Keep still," a soft voice urges, and I crack open my eyes.

The blue woman. I thought I imagined her. Her eyes are eerie—with vertically elongated pupils. She leans forward, and I feel my eyes widen as I take in the thin shirt covering what looks like three breasts.

"You helped me," I grind out.

"Yes. My name is Sonis."

"What's wrong with my leg?"

"The puncture wounds have been cleaned. However, there may be damage to your tendon."

I slump back on the lumpy pillow. I've damaged my tendon before. If it's bad, I'll have surgery as soon as I get home.

I lift my head slightly as cool hands touch my feet. Then they move away, and the woman slides another pillow beneath my head so I can see what she's doing.

"Your feet are in bad condition."

"Yeah, that's kinda how I roll."

She cleans and dresses the cuts on my feet and then brushes her fingers over the thickened skin on the tip of my toe.

"I'm a dancer," I say at the quizzical expression on her face.

She still looks confused, but she nods and then glances

toward the doorway. I turn my head and meet the gaze of the warrior who saved me.

My skin prickles with awareness, and despite the excruciating pain, my eyes travel over his body. He's huge and muscled, with longer hair than I'd usually expect to see on a man. His eyes are light brown, the expression on his face closed as he looks at me.

I clear my throat. "Thank you for helping me."

"I had no choice."

Well.

"You could've left me there," I point out, and he simply tilts his head slightly, his eyes narrowing as if I'm a particularly annoying kind of stupid.

"No warrior would leave a child or a female in such danger."

His voice is a low growl, and I nod, amused despite myself. "I'm sorry if I inconvenienced you."

He inclines his head but doesn't offer any platitudes, obviously missing the slight sarcasm in my voice. I'm in the most pain I've ever been in, but I feel a small smile cross my face at his grumpy demeanor.

"Why were you in that region alone?" he asks. "It's Voildi territory."

All amusement flees. "I was stolen from my planet with other human women and sold on a slave planet. We were then loaded onto a spaceship that crash-landed here. The Voildi convinced us they were rescuing us, and then a bunch of guys who looked like you appeared."

His face hardens the moment I mention the word *Voildi*, his eyes darkening until I almost shiver.

"While they were fighting, we were stolen by another pack of Voildi."

"How did you escape?"

"I knocked one of them out during a bathroom break and jumped into a river."

Is that a hint of respect I see in his eyes? He nods, looking at me consideringly. Our staring contest, however, is interrupted as Sonis leans forward and hands me some water.

I sip it down before gasping as I lift my head and the movement jostles my leg. Fire rips up my body, and I grind my teeth.

Sonis hands me another cup. "Drink this."

"I can't spend my whole time unconscious. I need to help the other women."

The huge alien leans forward. "It is dark. You can do nothing now. Rest."

"Bossy," I murmur as my eyes slide shut. "What's your name?"

A long pause, and then I feel him step closer, brushing my hair off my face.

"My name is Zarix."

CHAPTER FOUR

B eth

THE PAIN IS SLIGHTLY BETTER WHEN I WAKE, DESPERATE TO pee. I sit up and gasp. Okay, maybe the pain isn't much better after all.

My stomach lets out a long growl, and I turn as Sonis walks in again.

"You're hungry," she says. "I am not surprised. Do they not have much food on your planet?"

I blush. I've always been thin. Since puberty, I've been careful with what I put in my mouth. The days since we were abducted have been lean on food, and it's showing on my body.

"I had plenty of food," I mutter. She raises one eyebrow but hands me a plate. The scent of some kind of bread hits me, and my mouth waters, my hand shaking.

"Careful," she says, gently helping me sit up and lean against the wall.

I take a bite, so hungry that I now feel nauseous. But as I swallow, my stomach begs for more, and I shove the bread into my mouth.

Sonis hands me some more water and a piece of fruit. Within a few minutes, my stomach is full.

"I'll get you something else later. Small meals are best."

I nod. "Thank you for everything you've done for me. I'm sorry, but I have no way to repay you."

She tilts her head. "Zarix has been bringing us food for years whenever he happens to be in this area. After my mate died, I thought we would starve. You owe me nothing."

She turns away, and I lean back again while she bustles around the room. Finally, I can hold it no more.

"Um. Do you have a bathroom?"

Her face is blank for a moment, and then she nods in understanding. "One moment."

She disappears and then returns with the warrior— Zarix, I remember, taking in his huge form. His face is blank, but I narrow my eyes on him as he gently lifts me, and I could swear I see amusement in his dark gaze.

I gasp out a curse, and he freezes.

"I'm okay, keep going."

Frustration hits me as the pain rips through me. How am I going to find Ivy and Zoey if I can't even walk?

"You're upset." Zarix shifts his large frame so he can walk through the doorway, careful not to hit my leg against anything.

I tell him what I'm thinking, and he frowns as he walks down the short hallway.

"You think you will find them alone?" he asks.

"Either that, or I'll find help."

He tenses. "You would die within hours, female."

"Wow, you're such a charmer. How *do* you keep the ladies away?"

He glowers down at me and then opens the door to a small privy. He moves forward, likely about to place me on the toilet, and I shake my head.

"I've got this."

He shrugs but gently lowers me to my good leg, and I use my hands to balance against the walls before pulling down my thin pajama shorts when he closes the door.

I'd give almost anything for a shower.

My skin crawls as I think about all the strange bugs and germs that could be attacking my immune system right about now. When I lift up the corner of the bandage on my leg, I can see blood staining my skin. I shudder but get on with my business before washing my hands in the small sink when I'm finished.

I open the door, and Zarix lifts me into his arms, cradling me against his huge chest.

I'm already exhausted, and I sigh as I let my head drop against his shoulder. He pauses and then continues walking until he places me on the bed again.

"What time is it?" I ask.

"Almost dawn."

"I need to leave and get help."

"You would die," he says again, and I frown.

"I'm going to make those Voildi pay for what they did to us."

"Sleep, Beth. We will talk when you wake."

Zarix

I watch as the female falls back into a deep sleep, her long eyelashes resting against her cheek.

"Will you stay?" Sonis asks, and I shake my head.

"My mission is important. If I do not find out which tribe the Voildi are targeting, hundreds or thousands of Braxians could die, and the Voildi would be well positioned to take another tribe."

"Would you leave her here?"

Sonis's voice is bland, but I read between the lines. "You believe I should take her with me?"

"She will not stay here. Just like you, she has a mission. If the Voildi have others like her..." Sonis's voice trails off, and she glances away. Both of us have lost loved ones to the Voildi.

"She is weak. And small. And underfed. She'll slow me down."

Sonis smiles and pats my cheek, her slitted eyes lighting with amusement. "Perhaps slowing down is just what you need."

"We both know what happened last time I was responsible for a female."

Sonis sighs. "What happened to Hana wasn't your fault."

I frown at her. "I will go check my traps."

She sighs again but nods, leaning forward and pressing the back of her hand against Beth's forehead as she checks for fever.

The female looks tiny and weak while sleeping. But when she's awake, her eyes burn with a cool fire.

She meant every word as she promised vengeance against the Voildi.

I check my traps and bring back a small xyri. It will feed

all of us today, and Sonis will be able to use it for stew over the next few days along with the udazin I hunted earlier.

When I return, I find a spot to sit outside and sharpen my sword. I'm not at all surprised when a small form slips out of the hut and joins me on the large rock.

"Does your mother know you're out here?" I ask.

Javir shrugs. "Will you go away again?"

"Yes."

"Why? You should stay here."

"You know why."

"Because you have to kill all the Voildi." He bares his teeth, showcasing the gaps where his front fangs will grow in.

"That's right."

"Will you take the pretty female with you?"

"If she insists." I lean over and ruffle his hair, and he grins.

"She does," a female voice sounds, and I turn.

Beth is standing outside, her face pale as she balances on one leg. Sonis has found her a long stick from somewhere, and her knuckles are white where she clutches it, resting most of her weight on it.

I study her body, my eyebrow rising with reluctant respect. I would expect the female to be resting after such a wound.

"You have two choices," I say. "I can find a hunting party from my tribe and order them to take you back with them. You would be safe there."

She shakes her head. "What's the other choice?"

"I have a mission that involves the Voildi. If I'm right, it's likely that the same pack that took your friends are involved in the plan to attack one of the Braxian tribes."

"I'm going with you."

I eye her. "It will be dangerous."

"You don't get it. I got free. I may be hurt, but Zoey and Ivy are still with those bastards. They would come for me if I was the one left behind."

"If you're coming with me, you have to keep up. I don't have time to stop and coddle you."

She stares at me coolly. "I can keep whatever pace you set."

I sigh. Truthfully, I know Sonis is right. Beth will likely not stay here if I leave her. So I will take her with me and attempt to convince her to go with a hunting party when we find one.

"Sonis has a tub. I will fill it, and you may use it before we leave."

A blush heats her cheeks as she gazes down at her body. I've likely offended the female. But she nods, gratitude in her eyes. "That would be great. Thanks."

I clear my throat, looking away from the warmth in her eyes.

"You should go rest," I say.

She hesitates for one long moment and then turns, slowly making her way back into the hut.

Beth

Never again will I take clean water for granted. It seems to take forever to fill the bath, as the water has to be brought back, heated, and poured into the large tub. Sonis helps me maneuver myself into the bath, encouraging me to keep my injured leg out of the water.

"I stitched your flesh," she says. "Zarix knows how to remove the thread, and he will do it for you when it is time."

I nod, trying not to think about the risk of infection. At least I've had a tetanus shot. If that's even relevant on this planet.

"Thank you. For everything. Including this bath. The water feels amazing."

Her face softens, and she nods. "Let me know when you're ready to get out."

She turns, and I reach for the soap before lathering my hair and rinsing it twice. The water turns murky, and I make sure to wash the rest of my body before finally resting my back against the tub, exhausted.

I could use some serious painkillers right about now.

I can't complain though, knowing that Zoey and Ivy are still stuck with the Voildi. I wish we all could have escaped together. But since we didn't, I'm going to do everything I can to get them free.

Hopefully Zarix will cooperate.

I chew on my lip as I consider the giant warrior.

He's impatient and seems to be more annoyed by my presence than anything else. He's gruff but not cruel, and I feel my heart thump as I remember how he ruffled Javir's hair earlier.

The kid looks at Zarix like he's his hero. And Zarix tamps down his obvious impatience long enough to talk gently with a boy who is likely in need of a male role model.

I call to Sonis, and she steps in, helps me out of the bath, and hands me a long, wide piece of material to use as a towel.

"Thanks again," I tell her. "I can't even tell you how long it's been since I was clean."

She nods, a smile dancing around her mouth. "I left some clothes in your room."

After everything I've been through, it's comforting to know that there are good people on this planet. People like Zarix who would rescue an alien woman from a trap and Sonis who would tend to that alien's wounds and make her comfortable.

I use the cloth to squeeze the excess water from my hair and then wrap it around me, opening the door. I step out and freeze as I meet Zarix's gaze.

He gives me a long look, taking his time as his eyes run over my body. I blush as I feel my nipples peak, and his gaze snags on my chest before rising to my face.

His eyes are dark, and I catch one of his hands clenching into a fist before he returns his attention to his sword.

"You should eat before we leave," he says. "You're too thin."

I swallow and whirl, limping painfully into the bedroom. I grind my teeth as fire shoots through my leg, and I wish I had brought my walking stick with me.

Too thin.

Ballet dancers are supposed to look ethereal onstage. We need to be light so our partners can lift us. Our costumes leave nothing to the imagination, and we stare at ourselves in the mirror for hours at a time while we practice, wearing only a leotard.

Our bodies are continually examined, and it's easy to lose touch with reality, constantly thinking about what we're putting in our mouths.

I try to put myself in Zarix's shoes. He's huge and well-muscled, and he just went and killed a beast for Sonis, suggesting that food is in short supply. Maybe he thinks I've been starving, and—in his blunt, surly way—he's attempting to help.

It still stings. No woman wants to be told she's somehow lacking while she's wearing only a towel. And especially when those blunt words come from someone who radiates sexual charisma like Zarix.

I grind my teeth some more as I struggle into the clothes Sonis left for me. And then I replay the interaction in my head.

I'm well-versed in body language. I spent years ensuring I was perfectly in step with the other dancers in the corps. And the look in his eyes, combined with the way his hand had fisted...

My heart beats slightly faster at the thought of that large hand touching me.

Get a grip, Beth. You've got plenty of other stuff to focus on right now. Keep your head in the game.

I struggle uselessly with the back of the thin shirt. Cool hands take over, and I turn my head as Sonis deftly ties the strings holding it to my chest.

"I'm sorry. This is very large on you."

I shrug. "I guess I'm just a scrawny weakling on this planet." I laugh, but it must sound bitter because Sonis's hands pause.

"Zarix is...difficult."

I blush. She must have heard us talking a few moments ago. "Ignore me. I'm being a whiny baby."

She lets out a low laugh. "Some males speak before they think. Smart females will look beyond their words and to their actions."

I nod. Zarix may be blunt to the point of bordering on rude, but he also saved me in the forest, brought me here, and hung around even though he clearly has other things to do.

I change the subject, turning around to face her as she finishes with the shirt. "Your son is lovely."

She smiles, her blue face shining with love. "He is my pride and joy. Zarix is very patient with him." She glances away, and a rough sigh leaves her throat. "My mate was taken by a pack of Voildi three summers ago when we lived deeper within their territory. My friend used to trade with some of the Braxian women from Zarix's tribe, and she convinced me to ask Zarix's qatai for help. His tribe king," she tells me at my blank look.

"Did they help?"

She nods. "Zarix hunted the pack alone. I was furious at first, convinced that he was being arrogant and should have taken more warriors with him to face the monsters who took my mate."

"I'm guessing he didn't need them."

Her mouth twists into a wry smile. "No," she says softly, "he didn't. Zarix tore through the Voildi pack, removing all traces of them from this planet. Unfortunately, it was too late for my mate. He was severely wounded and died hours later."

"I'm so sorry."

She nods and wipes her face, her movements brusque. "We brought him home, and he spent his last hours with his family. That was more than I had even hoped for once he was taken."

"You live alone now?"

She nods. "My friend lives closer to Sebe, but I won't leave. This home is all we have, and we are close to the hut where my son completes his lessons. After Zarix destroyed the pack, he left the evidence for other Voildi to see, and word spread that to target us is to invite retaliation by the Braxians."

"You're very brave."

Sonis shrugs. "Do you have any children?"

"No."

"I have no choice but to be brave for Javir. He has already lost more than any child should have to lose."

She runs her gaze over my dress and nods, and we both smile as my stomach lets out a rumble.

She reaches over and hands me my walking stick. "Time for some food."

CHAPTER FIVE

Z arix

BETH IS QUIET AS SHE EATS, AND I FIGHT NOT TO PACE restlessly. We need to leave soon if we are to get to Sebe before dark. While the area is supposedly neutral territory, it would be stupid to travel with a female when the sun is down.

My hands fist at the thought. I work best alone. Now I will have to make allowances for this female. She is small, injured, and weak, and I don't have time to take her back to camp and resume my journey.

Beth's gaze meets mine, and she frowns as if she knows what I'm thinking. She stares at me for one long moment and then returns to her meal—root vegetables and meat from the udazin I hunted earlier.

I offended her when I told her she needed to eat. I could tell by the widening of her eyes, the slight twist of her mouth. I don't have soft words like other males, and if she imagines that I will whisper gently to her, she is wrong.

I have no desire to be responsible for another person's safety. Especially a tiny female's.

I get up and move into the cooking room before gathering the food that Sonis has kindly prepared for us to take. She gives me a small, wistful smile, and I know she wishes I was not leaving.

There have been many times that I have hunted for this female and she has attempted to convince me to stay.

"Take this. She will be in more pain soon and will need it."

I nod and take the waterskin, which Sonis has filled with her pain tonic. Beth appears behind me, and Sonis takes her bowl.

"Thank you," Beth says. "I was very hungry." She keeps her eyes off me, and I wonder if she is still grieved by my words from earlier. I shrug. The female has obviously been without food for some time.

Her body...while delicate, with the cloth wrapped around her, there was no doubt that she is a fully grown female. Her breasts, though small, are round and perfectly formed. Her hips, while narrow, curve gently, showcasing her tiny waist. And her legs...

I stifle a groan. The female is much shorter than Braxian females, yet her legs seem to go on forever. They were long and smooth in the dim light, pale and toned.

I turn away, striding for the door, and my voice is tight. "We are ready to leave," I say, and the females are silent for a moment.

"Jeez," Beth says. "Have you ever seen him smile? I bet his face would crack."

Sonis laughs and says something that I don't hear, and I

move outside to ensure the mishua is ready. I'm well aware that my face is hard, my body scarred, and my expression often stern. I am not a male who laughs and smiles with ease, which is one of the many reasons I stay away from camp, aware that my sour presence discomforts my tribemates.

I am sure Beth is well used to being surrounded by males that have wide smiles. Males that give her sweet compliments and make her laugh.

My mood is dark as I saddle the mishua. She nips at my fingers, and I give her a handful of feed. "You've already been fed," I tell her. "You'll feel unwell if you have more before we leave."

She snorts at me and seems to glare but swings her head, staring at Javir as he follows me from the hut.

"Can I come with you?"

"You know you can't."

He glowers at me. "You said one day I could. One day I would be a warrior like you. Why can't it be today?"

"I said this would happen when you were fully grown. You are still too young."

"Why does the female get to go with you? She doesn't know anything. She didn't even know what an udazin was."

He stamps his foot, and I stare. Javir is usually even-tempered—more likely to attempt to wheedle than to demand.

"The female needs to find her friends," I say, reaching for patience.

"I never get to go," he says. "I'm sick of being stuck here. I want to hunt the Voildi too."

Ah. That's what this is about. He has heard me and his mother talking.

I sigh. "You will. One day. You would be killed by the

Voildi if you were to hunt them now. Your father wouldn't want you to throw your life away."

"My father is dead," he says, his eyes filling with tears, and he glances away, refusing to let them fall.

"Then think of your mother," I say. "And do not make her mourn the last of her family."

He gazes back at me for a long moment and then turns and runs inside, almost crashing into Beth as she exits the hut.

"Javir!" Sonis snaps, but he ignores her, slamming the door behind him, and she widens her eyes at me.

"What was that about?" she asks.

"He wants to come with us." I reach for a small knife that I use to gut fish and cut fruit. "Give him this," I say, handing it to her. "Tell him that when I return, I will show him how to use it.

Sonis nods, and I catch Beth's soft smile out of the corner of my eye.

She moves closer to the mishua, gazing up at it as she chews on her lip. "I know I must have been on that thing on the way here, but it looks pretty scary from where I'm standing."

The mishua lowers her head, curling her lip to display sharp teeth, and Beth jolts back, using her walking stick for balance.

The movement seems to hurt because her face drains of color, and my mood darkens further.

"Stop moving," I snap, and Beth freezes as her eyes widen at my tone. I suppress a growl, and Sonis sends me a knowing look.

I lean forward and pick up Beth as she lets out a squeak, almost hitting me with the stick she uses to walk. Once she's seated on the mishua, I turn to Sonis.

"Thank you for your help," I say, and she smiles at both of us.

"Anytime. May the gods watch over your journey," she says, and I nod, casting one last look at the hut, but Javir is nowhere to be seen.

I swing myself up behind Beth and direct the mishua back toward the path while Beth waves at Sonis.

It's time to resume my mission.

Beth

Zarix is silent behind me while I fight to keep my calf from rubbing against the leather saddle. This is nothing like riding a horse.

This strange beast is scaled, yet it feels warm when I dare to touch its green skin. Lethal-looking horns protect every inch of its face and head.

"What's his name?" I ask.

"Her. Only female mishua can be ridden. The males are too wild. Her name is Rexi."

Rexi moves in an odd way, jolting me around on her back. Zarix has relaxed in the saddle, while I seem to be bouncing around like a Ping-Pong ball.

I attempt to keep track of the way we're going, and it's not long until we're back at the trap, which is still covered in my blood. I swallow down bile as Zarix jumps down before leading the mishua forward.

"What are we doing here?" I ask.

He ties Rexi to a tree and then deftly dismantles the trap. "I will ensure the Voildi cannot use this again."

"Thank you," I say as he moves back toward the mishua. "I wouldn't have been able to get free. You saved my life."

He nods, glancing away, obviously discomfited by my gratitude. I suppress a smile. This guy isn't big on feelings. Or talking. Or pretty much anything, it seems.

Zarix gets back on the mishua, and I feel his big body freeze behind me. He has tied my walking stick to the mishua, who didn't seem pleased, and I glance down, wondering if something has fallen off the saddle.

Then I'm being lifted again, and I yelp as Zarix moves me so I'm riding sidesaddle. He takes a blanket from one of the saddlebags and wedges it beneath my knee so my calf is in no danger of hitting the saddle or the mishua.

"Thanks," I say, and he nods stiffly, eyes focused ahead.

He seems to hate my appreciativeness, and I bite my lower lip to suppress a smile.

Mental note: When the giant alien tells me I'm scrawny, I can annoy him by thanking him for things. His dark gaze meets mine for the briefest moment, and he seems to read my mind because he scowls.

Then I'm bouncing along again, almost losing my seat at the new position. Zarix lets out a low growl and wraps his arm around me, pulling me closer to him. I glance up at him from beneath my lashes and frown at his blank expression.

In New York, the men I date are smooth, eager to please, charismatic, and funny. They're gentlemen, and they know how to navigate every possible social situation. Zarix? He's barely out of the cave. Stubborn and scowly, alternating between snapping at me curtly and attempting to ignore me completely.

So why do I find myself strangely drawn to this grumpy, rough warrior? Why do I find myself imagining what his hard face would look like if he smiled?

I push the thought from my head as we turn onto a slightly wider trail.

"Where are we going?" I ask.

"A place called Sebe."

I frown. Getting information from Zarix is like pulling teeth.

"Why are we going there?"

He sighs, and his breath tickles the back of my ear. I fight back a shiver.

"I believe the Voildi are planning to work together. Right now, even one or two packs wouldn't be enough to take the smallest Braxian tribe. But if they could cooperate, they could attack as one, slaughtering an entire camp and taking it as their own."

I shudder at the thought. "When I was with the Voildi, the leader mentioned that there aren't many females here and he had plans for us."

Zarix nods behind me, adjusting his arm and pulling me slightly closer as I wobble in the saddle. "If they weren't going to eat you, it's likely that they would be planning to sell you. There was a slave market in Nexia until my qatai found out about it and we destroyed it several summers ago. However, it's possible that it has been rebuilt."

I nod. "Where's Nexia?"

"Nexia is the area surrounding Sebe. We will look for any sign of your friends while I gather information about the Voildi's plans."

"Do you really think the Voildi could take one of your tribes?"

He adjusts his body in the saddle, and I resist the urge to lean against his hard chest.

"I think it is unusual that a pack of Voildi had the intelligence to think to sell you instead of simply using you as fresh meat. And I think if that pack can convince other packs to work with them, they could be a threat."

I mull this over. "I guess, all things considered, we're lucky we were taken by those Voildi. At least they were willing to let us live long enough to sell us. You called your people Braxians? How many tribes do you have?"

Zarix's chest brushes my back as he shrugs, leaning forward to adjust the mishua's course slightly. "There are many."

"Why don't you join together to fight the Voildi?"

He's silent for a moment. "Our tribes are very different. We have sometimes been forced to protect ourselves from other Braxian tribes who would take our resources for themselves."

I frown. This planet is scary. Not only are the Braxians at war with the Voildi, but they're fighting each other as well. The sooner I can get back to Earth, the better.

Time passes. I alternate between imagining what could be happening to Ivy and Zoey and reassuring myself that they're fine. While Zoey is injured, Ivy is a tough cookie. I know she'll do everything she can to get them both away from the Voildi. Maybe they've already managed to escape and they're somewhere safe and warm.

Or maybe the Voildi are watching them much more carefully now that I've managed to get away.

The thought depresses me, and I slump in the saddle as I yawn, still tired. We've probably been on this mishua for close to an hour, and its slow, steady pace is making me long for a nap. But Zarix seems just as fresh as the moment we left Sonis's, his eyes alert as he continually scans our surroundings.

I've tried not to think about how long I've been gone from Earth and what would have happened to my life since

I disappeared. I'm guessing I've been gone for around a week, although it feels like much longer. Are people looking for me? Do they know I've been taken? Or do they believe I couldn't take the pressure and ran away?

"What are you thinking?" Zarix asks in a low voice, and I raise an eyebrow, having not expected him to be interested.

"I'm thinking about my life. About what might have happened while I've been gone. And I'm wondering if my future and all of my dreams will have gone up in flames by the time I get back."

The thought makes me even more depressed, and I scowl. Why was *I* taken? Was it completely random? Or was it something that I did? How did I draw the attention of the Grivath? What could I have done to stay off their radar?

"What is your planet like?" Zarix asks, and I breathe through the homesickness that sinks into my chest, spreading through my body like a virus.

"Well," I say, glancing up at the sky, "my planet is called Earth. And the sky is blue."

Zarix is quiet for a long moment, and I turn my head, finding him frowning up at the green sky.

"I can't imagine that," he says, and I laugh.

"Yeah, it was a shock landing here."

"Is it difficult to hunt for food on Earth?"

I frown and then surprisingly, my mouth curls up in a smile. "No. We don't have to hunt. At least, not in most countries. In my country, we go to a supermarket. Imagine a huge building with every kind of food you can think of. We buy the food and take it home."

"But who hunts for that food?"

"The meat is raised in cages for the most part. Some of the animals live outside, but they're killed and butchered before they get to the supermarket."

Zarix grunts, and I can tell he's struggling with the idea. "You do not need to hunt, and you can eat as much food as you want. Yet you are thin, female. Very thin. Explain this to me."

I tense, cursing as the movement jolts my leg. The pain adds to my anger, and my tone is harsh as I turn, staring him in the eye. "I'm a dancer," I explain through my teeth. "I choose to make my body look this way so I can perform. But I'm fit and healthy."

Zarix examines my face for a long moment, his expression disbelieving. Then the mishua suddenly stops, and I clutch onto the strong arm wrapped around my waist.

The mishua turns her huge head, and I get a glimpse of one red eye narrowing as she gazes behind us. Zarix jumps from her back and draws his sword.

"Show yourself," he orders, and I hold my breath as a gray-blue bush shakes.

Then Zarix is cursing up a storm, only half the words being translated by the device in my ear as the spy steps forward.

CHAPTER SIX

Z arix

JAVIR STANDS, HIS HEAD BOWED AS I ROAR AT HIM.

"What were you thinking?"

"I wanted to go with you."

"And I told you no. Your mother will be terrified."

"I left her a note."

I grind my teeth. Javir is good at many things for his age, but his letters are not one of them. I will be surprised if Sonis can decipher whatever it is he has written.

But at least she will know that he has left of his own free will and wasn't taken.

If we return to Sonis, we won't make it to Nexia before dark. Another growl rips from my throat as I snarl down at the boy. He hunches his shoulders, and Beth clears her throat, raising one eyebrow at me.

"We will take him with us," I tell her, and Javir raises his head, hope in his gaze. I narrow my eyes at him. "But the moment I find a hunting party from our tribe, they will take him back to his mother."

He nods, staring back down at the ground, and I curse, turning away to pace. Not only do I have an injured female to protect, but now I have a child as well.

My fists clench at the reminder of the last time I was responsible for another person's safety, and I barely resist the urge to turn back and leave both Beth and Javir back at Sonis's.

I can't afford to lose any more time. If the Voildi are able to form alliances with each other, they could attack before I find the information we need.

"Get on the mishua," I grit out, and Javir turns away, unsuccessfully attempting to hide his relief.

He scrambles up behind Beth, and I mount the beast, who also seems displeased, tossing her head as she lets out a low growl.

"I feel the same," I mutter to her, ignoring the way Beth's mouth twitches. I move Javir behind me, instructing him to hold onto me. Then we're moving again, and I meet Beth's laughing gaze.

"I refuse to be responsible for him," I say, and Javir's hand tightens on my shirt.

"I can look after myself," he mumbles. "I'm smart."

"If you were smart, you would have stayed with your mother."

"I'm not a baby."

"The fact that you have to say that—"

Beth reaches back and squeezes my thigh, her hand warm. "He just wants to be like you," she says softly. "Although I can't possibly understand why." Her voice is teasing, and I frown down at her.

"I want to kill the Voildi too," Javir says. "I'm going to kill them dead with my knife."

I growl, and Beth turns her head, a smile playing around her mouth. She is injured and exhausted and has been taken from her planet, yet she still has the ability to smile.

I encourage the mishua to speed up, and she picks up the pace. Javir falls against me, and I reach back, pulling the knife from his hand.

"Hey!" he shouts.

"You'll get it back when you can be trusted."

"But—"

"Silence."

"That's not fair!"

Beth turns, narrowing her eyes at both of us. "Don't make me pull this car over," she says, and I tilt my head.

Her face is losing color, and she's tense in the saddle. I curse and slow the mishua. The faster pace is hurting her.

"What are you doing?" she asks.

Rexi turns her head, narrowing her red eye at me as if she's wondering the same thing.

"You are in pain," I say.

"I'm fine. We need to get there as soon as possible."

I reach into one of the saddlebags and pull out the pain tonic.

Her lower lip juts out, and I drop my eyes to her mouth. She blushes, and I scowl as I realize I'm staring.

"Take it," I say, my voice harsh.

"It'll make me sleepy."

"You can sleep against me. If you take it, we can travel faster."

The thought of getting to her friends more quickly obviously works because she takes a few sips with a grimace. Javir is quiet behind us, his head resting against my back, and I sigh, reaching behind me. I take a piece of rope from one of my bags and loop it into his belt before tying it to my wrist. Then I pull Beth closer and allow the mishua to increase her pace.

The sooner this mission is complete, the better.

BETH

ZARIX BECAME TENSER AND TENSER THE CLOSER WE GOT TO Nexia. It's clear that he's unhappy at the fact that he not only has me with him but now has to keep Javir safe as well.

I slept on and off while we traveled, and now I'm groggy, my calf aching. But it feels good to stand, even if all my weight is on one leg, and I stretch my back, leaning on my walking stick as Zarix takes care of the mishua, Javir shadowing his every step.

For a guy as grouchy as Zarix, he's surprisingly patient with Javir, who obviously worships him.

"What's the plan now?" I ask. I'm still out of it from whatever is in that pain medication, and I'd kill for a cup of coffee.

"Nexia is relatively neutral ground. Most species rely on the market to trade goods, but it's still dangerous here. There's a tavern close by, but we will need to be careful." Zarix looks at me and Javir, and I can practically hear him calling us liabilities in his head.

"I can help," I say, and he gazes at me for a long moment before finally nodding.

"This will be covert work. We need to find out anything we can about the Voildi packs and their plans. I will be meeting an acquaintance, but you should also listen for any helpful information."

I almost rub my hands together. Those Voildi bastards are going down.

Zarix reaches into his saddlebag and pulls out a long cloak before handing it to me. I pull it on, and he gestures for me to raise the hood.

"No one can know that you are a female," he says. "If the Voildi discover that you are the one who escaped..." His mouth firms, and he tilts his head as if once again weighing up the risks.

"I understand," I say quickly. "I'll hobble in with my walking stick and stay covered. They'll probably assume I'm an old man."

Zarix nods and glances at Javir. "And what are you going to do?"

Javir shrugs. "Stay silent?"

"Good."

Javir sends me a look, and I almost laugh. This kid is going to be trouble one day.

We leave the mishua tied to the tree. I almost ask Zarix if it's a good idea, but one look at the beast who seems like she could breathe fire, and I shrug. Anyone who attempted to steal her would be taking their life in their hands.

According to Zarix, there are hundreds of prexas—long underground tunnels that allow people to travel wherever they need to go without the risk of being surrounded. Thankfully we're already close to the market, which houses the large tavern where Zarix is meeting his contact.

The breeze rustles the leaves of the trees as we move out of the forest and walk down a wide dirt path. I tense as we pass a group of furred creatures, most of them around Javir's size. One of them sneers at him, and he hisses, brandishing the knife he must have pickpocketed from Zarix.

Zarix gives him a look and then heaves a long-suffering sigh but doesn't take the knife away.

"Behave," he orders as we walk. "Remember, don't draw attention to yourselves."

We both nod, and Javir sheepishly puts the knife away, his cheeks turning a darker shade of blue.

This part of Nexia is run down and old, the buildings leaning against each other, little more than shacks. And yet the sight of an honest-to-God town makes me breathe a sigh of relief. For some reason, it pleases me to know that this planet is more than just forests and caves, with the occasional hut here and there.

I'll be a city girl until the day I die.

I pull the cloak closer, trying not to hiss at the tiny amount of weight I put on my leg as I hobble along with my makeshift walking stick. Somehow I know without a doubt that if Zarix knew how much pain I was in, he'd insist I wait back with the mishua.

But I need to play a part in making the Voildi pay.

What would it have been like if Zarix and his tribe had found us on that ship instead of the Voildi? I have no doubt that they would have given us medical treatment and food. I blush as I remember the look on Zarix's face when I said he could have left me in the trap.

I'd insulted the huge warrior's honor.

It was men like him that attacked the Voildi in the clearing. So hopefully the other women are doing just fine right now and we'll all meet up as soon as I find Zoey and Ivy, and we can find a way to get back to Earth.

And I can try to rebuild whatever is left of my career.

We follow Zarix to the end of a long row of shacks, and

he gestures at one that's much larger than the rest. Creatures of all shapes and sizes are coming and going from the building, a few of them stumbling as they leave. Some give Zarix filthy looks, others nod at him, but all of them give him a wide berth while completely ignoring Javir and me.

Excellent.

The tavern is dimly lit, and it takes my eyes a moment to adjust as we enter. I feel my nose wrinkle, and I duck my head, checking once again that my hood covers most of my face. There are a few wooden stools here and there, but most people sit on overturned crates.

Everyone ignores us when we walk in, and even though Zarix's face is blank, I can sense some of the tension leaving his body. Obviously kids aren't an issue in bars here because Javir struts into the tavern as if he owns it.

Zarix gestures to a couple of crates in the corner, and Javir and I sit down, watching as Zarix moves to the long table that passes for a bar.

If a mishua had two legs and could talk, it would probably look similar to the scaled green man who takes his money.

I let my gaze travel over the crowd and tense as I spot a large group of Voildi on the opposite side of the room.

"There they are," Javir says. "Don't you wish we could just kill them?"

The words are hard and sound wrong coming from such a small kid. Javir smiles at my silence and sits up higher on the crate.

"They killed my father," he says.

I nod. "I know. Your mom told me. I'm sorry."

I almost tell him to stop staring at the Voildi because he's sure to draw attention to us, but he flicks his glance away, his face scrunched up with pain.

"They don't need to eat creatures that can walk and talk," he says. "There are plenty of beasts on this planet if you know how to hunt like Zarix and the other Braxians."

"So why do they do it?"

Javir shrugs, and we watch as Zarix moves back toward us.

"Maybe we taste better."

I grimace at the thought, and Zarix sits down, his crate creaking ominously under his weight.

The cup in his hand is short and squat and has been made from some kind of wood. I stare at it, fascinated. Is this what early cups looked like on Earth?

"What are you drinking?" I ask.

"Noptri," Zarix says. Then he tilts his head. "Would you like to taste it?"

I'm a dirty, dirty girl for the way my thighs clench at the way his low voice asks that question.

"Sure." I reach for the cup, and my fingers brush his hand. It's like a shock of electricity, and I almost gasp. He jerks his gaze to mine, tilting his head, and then pulls his hand away, turning back to the room.

I take a sip, and my eyes instantly water as I cough. It's like fire, burning down my throat.

Zarix turns back as I choke, taking the cup from my hand.

Granted, I'm not a big drinker at home. Dancers socialize with other dancers for the most part, our schedules too packed for many events. Most of us are much too disciplined to spend our few hours of free time drinking.

And I never wanted to risk the calories.

My cousin Rebecca is a social butterfly who can drink many of her guy friends under the table. But even she would struggle to drink this noptri stuff.

I watch Zarix as he drinks the noptri like it's water. "When will your contact be here?"

Zarix shifts, carefully avoiding looking at the Voildi in the corner. They're deep in conversation, and I eye Javir, who has turned his back on them, probably in an effort to ignore them.

The tavern is getting louder, a group of males raising their voices a few feet away, and Zarix leans closer to me.

"Someone will have told him I am here. It won't be long now."

I watch the Voildi while we wait, hiding under the hood of my cloak. One of them is dressed the same way as the Voildi who took us from the clearing, with most of his body covered in a thin cloth that could be mistaken for oversize pajamas. The others are dressed like the ones who discovered us on the ship and are wearing nothing more than loincloths.

Pajamas is talking while the others nod their heads. One of them reaches for his drink and glances toward us, his body going still as he stares at Zarix.

Zarix doesn't react, continuing to murmur to Javir, but I can tell from the muscle ticking in his cheek that the effort costs him.

The Voildi turns away and says something to the others, who glance over and sneer. I'm not a violent person, but the urge to stalk over and punch them in the face is almost overwhelming.

"I should get closer," I mutter. "Maybe I can learn something."

Zarix looks at me for a long moment and then finally nods. "Be careful. Here," he says, handing me a small metal coin. "Buy a drink."

I won't be drinking it, but he's right, I definitely need to blend in.

I'm not at all surprised when Javir gets up to follow me. Zarix reaches out a hand to pull him back, but the kid is too quick, and Zarix is obviously unwilling to make a scene.

"He's going to make you pay for that," I tell Javir, who shrugs.

We approach the bartender, who doesn't look up from the drink he's pouring.

"What do you want?"

"Noptri," I say, attempting to keep my voice low.

"One credit."

I hand over my coin and take my drink, turning to go. Javir stomps on my foot.

"Don't forget your change, uncle."

I nod and take the coins, and we move to a couple of crates closer to the Voildi. They don't look up, and I blow out a breath as we sit down. Okay, my leg is officially killing me.

"We need to get closer," Javir mutters. "I can't hear them over those guys."

He's right. The men next to us are arguing so loudly that they look like they're about to come to blows. They're the same race as Javir, and I study them, interested to see what he'll look like when he grows up.

One of them snarls, and I raise an eyebrow. Javir's baby teeth will be replaced with a mouthful of so many sharp teeth that they look like they couldn't possibly fit in such a small space.

Another male replies with clipped words and gets to his feet. I growl out a curse as Javir pulls my walking stick from my hand and slides it along the floor.

"What are you doing?" I hiss.

He ignores me, and I narrow my eyes. Zarix described Javir as nine or ten summers old, but he can't possibly be that young.

Maybe growing up on a planet as dangerous as this one just makes kids mature much faster.

Either way, the kid is reckless, and if he's not careful, he's going to get us killed.

The men are obviously inebriated because the one on his feet has spilled noptri down his shirt, leaving a wet mark. He sways slightly and then steps forward, and that's when Javir lifts the stick, sliding it beneath the guy's foot.

The man falls like a tree, his drink spilling all over his friend in the process. He hits the other man with his elbow, and that guy immediately swings his fist, hitting him in the jaw.

The first man goes down again, but this time he growls as he gets to his knees, teeth bared.

"Oh shit," I mutter. "Give me my stick, you little brat."

Javir grins at me but hands it over, and we move further from the group, as does almost everyone else. The move puts us closer to the Voildi just as the bartender gets to his feet.

"No fighting," he snarls. "Out!"

No one listens, and the bartender pulls out a crossbow.

"Oh shit. Get down!" I pull Javir to the floor, my vision graying as the movement jostles my leg. The bartender doesn't hesitate, firing a bolt into one of the men's legs.

I'm guessing that was a warning shot. And I don't want to know how much practice the bartender has had to make that shot.

The blue guy roars, but the bartender has already reloaded.

"Next one goes in your chest," he says. "Don't come back until your friend can hold his noptri."

The man pulls the bolt from his thigh and throws it at the bartender, who simply moves his head and lets it sail past him.

The men leave, one of them limping almost as bad as me. Across the room, Zarix stares at us, his face harder than I've ever seen it.

Yeah, he's not pleased.

I painstakingly begin the process of getting up from the floor.

"What," I mutter to Javir, "was that?"

CHAPTER SEVEN

Z arix

I REMOVE MY GAZE FROM JAVIR AND BETH, FIGHTING TO STAY seated and not drag Javir from this tavern by the scruff of his neck.

"Friends of yours?"

I return my attention to Tellou. "No."

He tilts his head as if he doesn't quite believe me but nods. He waves at the bartender, and I raise an eyebrow as the bartender waves back, stomping over to the corner to pick up the bolt for his crossbow.

Tellou doesn't bother to order a drink. His race processes noptri too quickly, feeling no effect from the strong liquid. Likely why his cousin is employed as a bartender here.

I lay a handful of coins on the table. "What do you know?"

Tellou glances down at the coins and then up at my face.

"What you had anticipated is coming true." He gestures to the Voildi on the opposite side of the tavern.

"They're joining together," I say.

He shrugs. "Maybe forever, maybe just for this event. Either way, it's guaranteed to shake up the power structure around here."

I clench my teeth. "You say that like it's a good thing."

He shrugs again, green shoulders rolling, and I let out a low growl at the dismissive movement.

"Maybe it's time someone took the power from the Braxians. You walk around here like you own this planet simply because the gods made you bigger and stronger than anyone else."

"We don't hurt innocents. The Voildi kill males, females, and children. They tear families apart."

He shrugs. "The Voildi may be a problem for you guys, but they leave us alone." He gives me a toothy smile. "Apparently they don't like the way we taste."

"Are you going to tell me what I need to know?"

He looks at me for a long moment. "For the sake of our friendship, I will tell you this. They're planning to hit Tecar's tribe first."

I grit my teeth. Tecar's tribe is small, and while our tribe has no trade agreement with Tecar, our sentries have been known to cooperate, sharing information about potential threats.

Tellou leans forward and pushes the coins toward me. "Sorry, Zarix, but they paid me more. And they offered protection."

I snarl as he gets to his feet, calling across the bar to the Voildi.

"This is him," he says. "This is Dexar's spy."

"Traitor," I bite out, reaching for him, but it's too late. He dances away, heading for the door.

"Sorry," he says, his mouth turned down as regret flashes in his eyes. "I have to do what's best for my people."

"You'll pay for this," I vow, and he nods solemnly as the Voildi get to their feet.

"Perhaps. Perhaps we will meet again, old friend. But you'll have to live through these next moments first."

The Voildi stalk through the tavern, separating as they dodge crates and tables.

Javir stands on his crate, his face losing color as one of them pushes past him, intent on my death.

I almost laugh. Tellou has known me for many years. Yet he still somehow has no idea who I am.

Unlike others, I don't spend my downtime at camp tumbling and drinking when I am not on a mission. I return to speak to Dexar, perhaps staying for a night or two. And then I leave, either on a new mission or to hunt for the tribe and track the Voildi.

For eight years, I have honed my skill with a sword. It will not be these Voildi that kill me this day.

Although, I have never had a female and a child to protect before.

The first Voildi reaches me, and I draw my sword.

He lunges, but he's slow. I slide away, cursing as my back hits the wall. Fighting in such confined conditions is difficult for a male of my size. I cut him down and step aside as patrons rush for the door, desperate to flee the violence.

There are six or seven Voildi left, and I flick my gaze behind them to where Beth and Javir are hugging the wall.

"I said no fighting!" the bartender roars, lifting his crossbow.

Beth jolts toward the bartender, her pained shriek

sounding as she uses her bad leg for speed. The noise carries over the panicked screams of the crowd as they vacate the tavern, and I clench my fists.

The bartender aims at me as another Voildi attacks, and I step aside, twisting to use the Voildi as a shield. The bolt goes through his throat, and I drop his body, distracted again by the female and child.

Beth swings her walking stick, hitting the bartender in the back of the head. She grabs the crossbow as he falls to his knees, and Javir picks up the bag of bolts lying close by.

The Voildi in the strange clothes turns at the commotion just as Beth hands Javir the crossbow, her hood falling from her head as she turns to me.

"Female," the Voildi hisses, and I clench my teeth as two others of his kind attack me as one.

Beth

Zarix is surrounded, his back to the door. He could easily slip out and give himself room to fight, but I know him well enough by now to know he won't leave us alone.

One of the Voildi has turned to me, his teeth bared. He looks a lot like the Voildi from the pack that I escaped from, although I don't recognize his face.

"We're in deep shit," I mutter, and Javir nods next to me. Zarix is currently fighting two Voildi at once. The one advantage he has is that while the space is obviously small for his huge body, the Voildi are forced to give each other space as well and can't all attack at the same time.

At least they can't right now. From the look on his face as he meets my eyes, he's planning something stupid.

Something stupid like crossing through the Voildi to get to us.

If we can't get to him, he's going to put himself at risk to protect us.

I see why he was so unhappy about us tagging along for this ride. We *are* liabilities.

"Can you see another way out of here?" I ask Javir. His face is pale, sweat rolling down his temples.

We both turn, scanning our surroundings while the Voildi in the strange clothes ignores Zarix, moving closer to us.

No doors. No windows on this side. We're trapped.

"Haven't these people ever heard of fire codes?" I snap while the Voildi pulls a long knife from behind his back and eyes Javir like he's a tasty meal.

One year, before my father had accepted the fact that all I wanted to do was dance, he insisted I go to a regular summer camp. There were tears and tantrums as I tried to bargain with him, desperate to go to ballet camp.

Even my mother couldn't reason with him.

"Honey," she'd finally said, "life can't just be about dance. You never know what other skills you'll learn that you might find helpful one day. Plus, you might even make some new friends."

I learned two things that summer. One, that I didn't want any friends that didn't understand how important ballet was. And two, that if there were a parallel universe where I could devote my life to more than one thing, that second thing would probably be archery.

Something about the feel of the bow in my hands, the graceful path of the arrow, and the thunk as it hit the target...it made me feel powerful.

Well, maybe this is a parallel universe.

I snatch the crossbow out of Javir's hands, my own hands trembling as I pick it up, aiming it at the Voildi.

The crossbow seems almost medieval, but it thankfully has a mechanical trigger and a magazine stocked with bolts. That means that even someone of my size can use it, and it won't take me precious minutes to reload it.

The Voildi stops in his tracks, tilting his head. Behind him, Zarix dispatches another Voildi, kicking one away as he meets my gaze.

"Fire!" Zarix roars, and I squeeze the trigger, my hands automatically responding to the command in his voice.

Somehow, for the first time since I was stolen from Earth, luck is on my side. The bolt hits the Voildi in the gut, and he shrieks as he folds, immediately pulling it out.

"Ooh, bad move, dude. Everyone knows that if you're impaled, the object stays *in*."

He bares his teeth at me but drops to his knees. Faster than I could have imagined, Javir jolts forward, slashing his knife across the Voildi's throat.

"Javir!" I gag as blood spurts, and his wide chin sticks out stubbornly, the look in his eyes much too adult for his young face.

Okay. We'll worry about the psychological trauma—both his and mine—later.

The bartender stirs, and I scowl at him as his eyes open to enraged slits.

"Do I have to shoot you too?"

His lips thin, but he shakes his head, groaning at the movement.

I turn as Zarix roars again, his sword sliding into a Voildi like a warm knife through butter. There are still two left, and Javir and I inch closer, stepping around bodies. Zarix is awe-inspiring, this massive, furious warrior, and I take a single moment to admire him before I pull Javir closer to the wall.

I hand Javir my walking stick and load the crossbow, but I can't get a clean shot. It's pretty likely that my first shot was a fluke, and chances are high that I'll hit Zarix by mistake.

One of the Voildi stumbles, and Zarix turns, kicking the other Voildi in the gut. Javir drops my stick, knife in his hand as he leaps forward.

"No!" Zarix snaps, but it's too late, and the Voildi grins as he raises his sword.

Then Zarix is there, pushing Javir away, and the Voildi's sword slips into his side even as Zarix takes off his head.

"Oh my God." I lurch forward, gritting my teeth as my eyes water with pain, and I pull Javir out of the way.

Zarix pulls the knife free and uses it to gut the other Voildi before sliding it across the first Voildi's throat.

"Fuck." I jump forward. "Are you okay?"

"Yes." Zarix runs his gaze over my body and then glowers at Javir. "What were you thinking?"

To his credit, Javir seems remorseful, his lower lip trembling as he takes in Zarix's wound. For the first time, he looks like the child he is. "I'm sorry."

Zarix's scowl deepens. "You could have been killed." He moves toward the door and stumbles.

"Hey," I say. "Absolutely not. Sit down. Now."

"We don't have time—"

"If you pass out, we're all screwed. Sit your ass down and let me take a look."

Zarix stares at me for a long moment and then finally complies, slumping onto a crate with a sigh.

"Does no one know basic first aid on this planet?" I snap as I stare down at his wound. "Impaled objects stay in!"

To my surprise, the corner of Zarix's mouth curls up. It

could never be mistaken for a smile, but it's the closest expression to it that he's made yet, and I blink at him. Something flutters in my stomach, and I turn my attention back to the bleeding.

"I know nothing about medicine," I say. "For all we know, he could have hit some important organ or something. We need to put pressure on it."

Javir begins searching through some of the bags left behind in the tavern, a few of them likely belonging to the dead Voildi. I give him a hard stare as he pockets a few coins, and he shrugs but doesn't put them back.

I sigh but give him a nod of thanks when he finds a relatively clean piece of material and a rope.

This is what my life has come to. Treating the wounds of an alien warrior with what looks like someone's shirt and a rope. Oh, and trying to convince a bloodthirsty child not to kill anyone else.

That reminds me.

I press the shirt against Zarix's side, taking his hand and pushing it against the wound. "Hold that tight."

Then I turn back to Javir and give him a hard stare.

"Hand it over," I say, and he doesn't ask what I'm talking about. His jaw juts out stubbornly again, but he glances back at Zarix's wound and then sighs, pulling out his knife and offering it to me.

The knife seemed tiny in Zarix's hand, but it seems huge in Javir's.

"Wipe it first," I hiss, shuddering at the blood, and he rolls his eyes but walks over to one of the dead Voildi before leaning over and swiping it along the Voildi's shirt.

I'm not a parent. I know nothing about children, but surely kids shouldn't be killing Voildi. No matter their species.

Zarix gets to his feet. "We need to go. Now."

I nod and reach for my walking stick. My leg is sticky with blood. My blood. I've definitely torn open some of my stitches.

Nothing I can do about it right now.

I grab my new crossbow along with a small canvas bag filled with bolts. Finders keepers. I don't even feel bad about it, since the bartender would have taken Zarix down without a thought.

It's getting dark as we make our way out of the tavern. Word has obviously spread about the fight because the area is almost empty. Zarix weaves, slightly unsteady on his feet.

"Lean on me," I say, and he shakes his head.

Stubborn male. We slowly shuffle back toward the forest, and we're almost there when Zarix stops in his tracks.

"I can smell blood," he says. "Blood that's not mine." He runs his eyes over Javir and me.

I scowl. No way his nose is that good.

"I think I ripped a few stitches," I say. "It's fine."

He glowers at me, jaw jutting out, the uncompromising look on his face so like the look Javir gave me when he killed the Voildi that I throw up my hands.

"Save me from stubborn males. Of all species," I mutter. "Look, standing around here isn't going to help anything. We need to get to the mishua."

He finally nods and then stumbles, almost dropping to his knees.

Javir moves in front of him, his face straining with the effort to hold up the Braxian. I limp closer and pull Zarix's arm around my shoulders, the height difference between us making it awkward.

"Put your hand on Javir's shoulder," I order, panic making my voice reedy and thin. If Zarix goes down, I have no idea what we'll do. For the first time, I'm realizing just how much I'm relying on the huge warrior to keep us safe.

And all we've done is gotten him seriously injured.

The walk through the woods feels like it takes hours, the sky darkening to a forest-green color. I clench my teeth, my jaw aching with the effort of not crying out at the pain.

This pain isn't simply from the stitches tearing. This is a deep pain. I've been pushing this knowledge away, unable to face it, but that doesn't make it any less true.

The trap hurt, but it was likely the fall that did the most damage—when my body went one way and my leg stayed in place.

On Earth, I probably would've had surgery by now. I'd at least have had it x-rayed and examined by a professional. I'd be resting until I could embark on a painful journey of strengthening and physical therapy. What I wouldn't be doing is walking around on it, running, or balancing the weight of a seven-foot-tall male.

The rule? Do nothing to make your injuries worse.

I laugh hollowly, and Javir turns to me, his eyes widening, likely at my grim expression.

I turn my attention back to our current situation. If we can't get on the mishua and out of this area, the possibility that I'll never dance again will be the least of my worries.

CHAPTER EIGHT

B eth

I stare up at the mishua, feeling like I'm gazing at Mount Everest. Zarix removes his arm from around my shoulders and holds it out.

"Up," he says.

"Um." I stare at him. If he lifts me, he's going to bleed even worse. And yet there's no way I can climb up alone.

Javir scrambles up on the other side of the mishua and holds out his hand. "Let him lift you just enough to reach my hand."

I nod, swallowing around the lump in my throat as Zarix pushes me up. My walking stick hits the mishua, and she lets out a low growl.

"Sorry," I mutter as I grab Javir's hand.

He's surprisingly strong for his size, and he helps me slide up behind him.

"Wow," he says. "You should eat more."

"Don't start," I warn him, and Zarix snorts from below us.

His eyes meet mine for a brief moment, the tiniest spark of amusement in them, and then he looks up at the mishua as if summoning his strength.

He hauls himself up, and I reach into the saddlebag for the pain tonic.

He shakes his head. "No," he says. "You take it."

"I'm not taking it," I say, and Zarix shrugs, apparently unconcerned as Javir slides behind him.

I grit my teeth as the mishua starts to move. "Where are we going?"

There's no reply from behind me, and Zarix's head has slumped onto my back.

"He passed out," Javir says, his voice slightly panicked.

"Oh God…"

The mishua stops in her tracks, and I scowl down at her. What now?

"Mishua don't allow females to ride them," Javir says. "She can probably tell Zarix isn't directing her."

I shove down the urge to let rip with the kinds of curses that shouldn't reach his ears. *Okay, think, Beth.*

"You're a male. Get up front and take over."

"You think she'll let me?"

"I think if she doesn't let you, we'll tie her to a tree and leave her for the Voildi."

The mishua lets out a weird groaning sound but thankfully begins walking once Javir grabs the reins.

"Do you know how to get back to his tribe?" I ask.

Javir shakes his head, and fear makes my hands tremble. I can't be responsible for this stern, gruff warrior dying. Not just because I seem to care more about him than I should but because he's actively attempting to stop a war.

"Okay, new plan. Do you know where to find anyone who would help us?"

Javir pauses and then turns his head, excitement clear on his face. "My father used to take me with him sometimes when he'd come to buy and sell goods in the market. Usually, there would be a couple of Braxian warriors near one of the prexas. I don't know which tribe they're from though."

I nod. "Do you know how to get there?"

"I think so."

"Then let's do it. It's our only shot."

The mishua speeds up slightly at my words, and I wonder how much she understands. Does she realize Zarix could be dying right now?

Zarix lets out a rough growl, and I reach back, taking his hand. His skin is cool. Not a good sign.

"It's okay," I tell him. "Hang on. We're going to find help. Just don't do anything stupid like die on us in the meantime."

He's silent, and I sigh, turning my gaze forward. Javir, on the other hand, doesn't seem to know the meaning of the word *silent*.

"So," he says, "why were you alone in Voildi territory anyway?"

I'm so tired that it takes me a moment to understand what he's asking. It feels like it has been years since I was running through the forest, desperate to find help.

"I escaped the Voildi, and I was trying to find someone to help me save my friends."

"The Voildi found my father when he was out hunting one day. My mother thinks the pack had been watching him for a few days first. Were you taken from your camp?"

"We were all stolen from different places on our planet," I say. "It's called Earth."

Javir whips his head around to look at me, his eyes wide. "For real?" he asks, and he sounds so much like a kid on Earth that in spite of our dire circumstances, I can't help but laugh.

"For real," I nod. "My planet is very different from yours. We don't live in camps. Some people even live in tall buildings, thousands of times bigger than the tavern."

"Are you playing with me?"

I laugh again. "I'm not."

"Why were you stolen?"

I sigh. "Believe me, I've been asking myself the same thing every day. I think sometimes terrible things happen to good people. I used to believe that bad things would always eventually happen to bad people, but I thought I was a good person."

Javir's voice is low. "My father was a good person."

I wince, attempting to tread carefully. I'm exhausted, and I don't want to blurt out anything that could further upset a boy who's still mourning his dad.

"Yeah. I think sometimes bad things happen for no reason. And it's unfair. But all we can control is how we react to those bad things."

It's going to take me some time to believe this myself. To allow myself to get past the fact that everything I worked for—all the years of training, the homeschooling so I could attend more classes, missing out on rites of passage like prom and homecoming—was all for nothing.

But eventually I'll need to come to terms with it. If I get home and I really can't dance again, or worse—and this is something I can hardly bare to think—I don't get home at all, I need to be able to move on with my life.

"Look," Javir says suddenly, jolting me from my thoughts.

I focus on the distance as Javir pulls the mishua to a stop. Between the trees, sitting on their own mishua while they talk amongst themselves...

Three Braxian warriors.

Zarix

Beth's words ring in my ears, and I manage to lift my head from where I've been resting it on her back.

"I think sometimes bad things happen for no reason. And it's unfair. But all we can control is how we react to those bad things."

Am I one of the bad things that happened in her life? Does she count this entire planet as a "bad thing"? I push that thought away.

This female is more pragmatic than I thought. From the pain in her voice, she has lost more than I could have imagined, yet from the moment she opened her eyes in Sonis's hut, she has been relentlessly focused on moving forward.

While I'm still looking back.

I pant through the pain as the mishua comes to a halt. Beth tenses slightly as I rest my chin on her shoulder, and then she relaxes, raising her hand to pat my cheek.

"It's going to be okay," she assures me. "Do you know those guys?"

I narrow my eyes at the warriors as they notice us and move closer. "They are from my tribe."

My chin almost falls off Beth's shoulder as she slumps in relief. Within moments, Tazo is by my side.

He curses as he looks at me. "What happened?"

"Knife meets guts," Beth says in a small voice. "We need to get him back to the healer."

"You are a human female," he says suddenly, taking her in, and she gasps as his eyes widen.

"You've seen others like me?"

He nods. "Our qatai bargained with Rakiz's tribe for one of the females they found."

I don't need to see Beth's face to know that her lips are likely thinning at this declaration, and her voice is sharp as she angles her head, her soft hair rubbing against my face.

"Bargained?" Her voice is like ice, and Tazo glances at me. "Forget it," she says. "How fast can we get him back to your tribe?"

Perik clears his throat as he rides closer, and I attempt to ignore the way Dekir—the third warrior—is staring at Beth in fascination.

"We are at least a day's journey from our camp," Perik says. "We can shave off a few hours if we go at full pace, but..." His voice trails off as Tazo glares at him.

"We will make it," Tazo says, and I meet his gaze for a brief moment. We have not spoken for years. But somehow, if I am to die, it seems right that it will be while he is with me.

After all, I am responsible for the death of his sister.

Tazo's brow lowers as if he's reading my mind, and then he turns to Beth. "Don't worry, female. This warrior is much too stubborn to die."

She snorts. "Okay. Let's go, then."

Javir moves onto Perik's mishua, and Tazo reaches for Beth, helping her sit in front of him. The color fades from her face at the movement, and I reach for the saddlebag, almost falling from the mishua.

Dekir reaches out to steady me. "What do you need?"

"Pain...Beth."

"Don't be ridiculous," she snaps. But I open my eyes, unaware they had slid shut.

"What's he talking about?" Tazo asks.

"He has a pain tonic in his saddlebag. We should force it down his throat."

Tazo is silent for a long moment.

"We don't allow females to be in pain when it can be prevented," he says, and I tense.

He curses roughly. "Zarix," he starts, but I close my eyes again.

His voice hardens. "Take the tonic, female. Zarix is well used to basking in his pain."

Beth is silent, but from the slight gagging noise she makes, I can tell she has taken a sip.

Something nudges my arm, and I manage to force my heavy eyes open.

She's pushing the tonic at me. "Now you," she insists, her eyes damp. "Please."

I sigh but take it, swallowing a gulp.

Dekir ties me to the mishua, and I rest my head on her scaly skin.

"Okay," Tazo says grimly. "Let's go."

***

Beth

It feels weird to sit in front of Tazo on the mishua after getting used to Zarix's strong arm clamped around my waist. Tazo is a perfect gentleman, but I miss the surly, short-tempered male currently unconscious and slumped over the mishua.

I can't even explain why.

The sight of him in so much pain...

It makes me want to cry.

This guy saved me from certain death and then only got stabbed because I wasn't paying enough attention to Javir.

"He's going to be okay, right?"

Tazo is silent for a long moment. "We have excellent healers," he finally says. "Some of the best on Agron."

I don't point out that he didn't agree with me.

We've been traveling for hours—long enough that dawn is stretching golden fingers over the huge empty space in front of us. I passed out for most of the night, something I'm grateful for, as it's currently a very bumpy ride.

"This will be the most dangerous part of our journey," Tazo tells me. "We will be fully visible to anyone lying in wait, and we don't have time to fight off a pack of Voildi. This will need to be fast."

I nod. "I'm ready."

With a glance at the other warriors, Tazo nods, and then I'm clutching onto him for dear life as the mishua takes off.

It's as if she suddenly has wings.

I hope Zarix is able to hold on tight to the mishua and he hasn't passed out again. We travel like this for a few minutes, and by the time we reach the tree line, I'm panting.

To think that I once thought I wanted more excitement in my life.

The sun is up, with not a cloud in the emerald sky, when Tazo slows his mishua to a walk. In the distance, a huge structure looms over many other smaller structures.

"What's that?" I ask.

"Our qatai's kradi," Tazo says.

Huh. If the qatai is the king, then that massive, sprawling tent must be his palace.

It has to be close to the size of a football field, and my mouth drops open as we get closer and I take in the sheer size of the camp. Thousands of smaller tents cover a huge distance, stretching almost as far as my eye can see. There must be tens of thousands of people living here.

A warrior approaches on a mishua, his eyes widening as he stares at Zarix.

"Prepare the healers," Tazo snaps, and the warrior immediately turns as we follow him through the camp.

I'm not sure what's going on between Tazo and Zarix, but I can tell for sure that there's some bad history there.

We make our way to one of the larger tents, close to the massive structure that's bigger than anything I've seen on this planet.

Tazo helps me down off the mishua and hands me my walking stick. Somehow he's kept it safe on our bumpy ride. Then the warriors untie Zarix from the saddle and haul him into the tent.

Javir's feet hit the ground as he jumps down beside me, and his hand shakes as he gives me my crossbow.

"Is he going to be okay?" His voice is small, and I don't tell him I'm wondering the same thing.

"You heard his friend. He's too stubborn to die."

Javir nods, but his face is still serious. "This is my fault. I did this."

I sigh. "You made a mistake. You acted before you fully thought about the consequences of distracting him. That Voildi saw what you did to his friend. He was luring you into a trap."

"Zarix could die."

"He could. But he wouldn't want you to blame yourself. You did something stupid, and now you get to learn from it."

Javir just glances up at my face and walks away.

"That was what he needed to hear," a deep voice says, and I turn.

A man is standing a few feet away, surrounded by warriors. His face looks like it has been formed out of rock, his nose crooked and his hair braided back from his face. He smiles, and the effect is charming, his full lips softening his face as he steps closer.

"I'm worried about him," I say.

He nods. "I will have my people watch him. He can have the illusion of space for now."

Strangely, the way he says that sentence makes me want to smile.

"Thank you."

"I am Dexar, the qatai of this tribe," he says, and my eyes widen. *Oh wow.* This guy is the king. I feel the sudden urge to curtsy, and I tamp it down.

Instead, I nod. "I'm Beth."

"Thank you for helping bring Zarix home."

My eyes fill with tears, and I blink them away. "I'm partly responsible for his injury," I say. "It was the least I could do."

He raises one eyebrow, the movement oddly elegant. I expected him to move like a brawler, but he prowls like a leopard as he moves closer. The light hits his eyes, and I'm suddenly reminded of the green sky on this planet as the sun goes down.

"I will attempt to talk to Zarix now," he says. "The information he has is crucial."

"Can I come with you?"

He nods and gestures me ahead of him. We move into the tent, which is much larger than it appeared from outside. I count ten beds at first glance, and the healers have surrounded Zarix, who lies shirtless on the bed furthest from the entrance.

Along his upper chest and shoulders is the same shimmery blue-green pattern I noted on the warrior with the ripped shirt in the forest. From here, they definitely look like scales, and I have the strongest urge to run my finger over them.

Get your mind out of the gutter, Beth. The poor guy's on death's doorstep.

"He is conscious now, qatai," one of them says, and Dexar steps forward. I follow in his footsteps as he moves closer to the bed.

"Zarix," he says, and the warrior opens his eyes to slits.

"Tecar's tribe is the first targeted," he grinds out. "But that information can't be trusted. Tellou turned on us."

Dexar's eyes darken dangerously, and I shiver.

"Just Tellou? Or all of his people?"

Zarix's brow lowers in a deep scowl. "All of them. They believe they will fare better under the Voildi. Their people are not hunted for meat, so they have chosen to take their chances as the Voildi's allies."

Dexar nods. "Anything else?"

Zarix glances at me. "Her leg. She needs a healer." He winces at something the healers do to him, and I blow out a steady breath, forcing myself to keep my eyes on his face.

I don't think that's what Dexar was referring to, but he nods.

"Recover well, Zarix," he says. "We will need you."

Dexar gestures to one of the healers, a Braxian woman with long dark hair, and she smiles at me.

I don't want to leave Zarix's side, but his eyes have

already slid closed. I push away the urge to nestle close, hold his hand, and whisper encouraging words in his ear.

Whoa. I'm obviously so tired that I've slid into crazy territory.

"My name is Elliz," the healer says.

"I'm Beth."

I turn and follow Elliz, who has me lie on another bed. She begins to gently take Sonis's bandages off my leg, and I close my eyes as her hands still.

Yeah, my guess is that it's not looking good.

My eyes are hot as I lie still. She does something that makes me cry out, and I turn my head, opening my eyes as a low, furious growl sounds from Zarix's bed.

The healers frown and glance at me.

"I'm sorry," I say, suppressing a yelp as Elliz does something else particularly torturous.

I meet her eyes, which are sympathetic as she glances at my face. Then she pours something on my wound, and I lose all control as a scream rips from my throat.

I writhe in pain, attempting to breathe through the agony. Commotion on the other side of the tent has me turning my head, and I gape as Zarix sits up suddenly, snarling.

The healers shriek, jumping back from him, and I gasp as the blue-and-green scales on his chest turn so dark that they appear almost black.

"Give her something for the pain!" he roars, and Elliz flinches. I don't bother protesting. For one, I'm close to sobbing, and from the fury on Zarix's face, he's not going to rest and let the healers work until I do what they say.

Elliz hands me a cup, and I gulp at the bitter liquid. There's obviously no fake fruit flavors on this planet, and I pinch my nose shut as I drink some more.

Zarix stares at me for one fraught moment, and I give him a shaky smile. He lies back down, and the healers slowly move back to his side, all of them wide-eyed. I feel a pang of annoyance, and I almost snap at them. He's just a man, for Pete's sake. They're acting like he's a monster.

Elliz waits until my shoulders hit the bed, and the world begins rotating around me in lazy circles. Then she gets back to work as my eyes slide shut.

CHAPTER NINE

B^{eth}

I MUST ONLY SLEEP FOR A FEW HOURS BECAUSE THE TENT IS still dark when I open my eyes.

I jolt when I meet Zarix's gaze. He's standing next to my bed, his face hard as he looks down at me.

"Were you watching me sleep?" I ask, my voice hoarse.

He nods silently, and I feel my eyes widen.

"That's creepy, dude." I'm joking, but he ignores me, still studying my face.

"Your actions saved my life," he tells me.

"Yeah," I say, and my lips twist as I glance away. "But let's be real—I'm part of the reason you were hurt."

He shakes his head, and I blink up at him as he leans closer. I almost gasp as I finally recognize the look on his face.

Desire.

He *does* want me.

He leans closer, and the moment stretches as we look into each other's eyes.

Finally, I snap.

I lift up my hand, slide it around his neck, and pull him down to me.

He meets my lips, and I groan, driving my hands into his hair as his mouth slams down on mine. There's nothing tentative about it. Nothing gentle. Nothing sweet. It's just pure need.

My mouth opens, and his tongue sweeps in, savagely claiming me. I groan, and he tenses, his whole body shaking. I reach for him as he pulls away, but he simply strokes his hand down my face, looks at me for another long moment, and then turns back toward his own bed.

Leaving me to growl in frustration.

I fist my hand and glare in his direction, but he's closed his eyes.

"You're not asleep, you big faker," I mumble. But I close my own eyes, sliding straight into sleep.

When I wake up next, I sigh as something cool touches my brow. I crack open my eyes, wincing at the light.

Elliz gazes down at me solemnly.

"How bad is it?" My voice is hoarse. How long was I out for?

"You will walk without a limp one day," she says, and I feel the strangest urge to laugh. That's it?

She tilts her head at my silence. "I have resewn the wound, and I also gave you an elixir to prevent fever."

I raise my eyebrows. Infection. She's talking about preventing infection.

"Thank you. I really appreciate it. How long have I been asleep?"

"Three days," someone says, and I turn at the sound of Zarix's deep voice.

He's still lying on the same bed, although someone has changed his pants. I glance down. In fact, someone has changed me too. I smell a lot better than I did.

I blush. Someone definitely gave me a sponge bath.

Elliz places a couple more pillows under my head as I stare at Zarix. His face is still pale, but he doesn't look like he's about to die anytime soon.

"Three days? Where's Javir?"

Zarix nods toward another bed, and I fight back a smile. Javir is curled into a ball, his knife clutched in his small fist.

"The little brat stole that knife back from me," I say right as the brat opens his eyes and grins.

Elliz smiles at me and moves away, and moments later, Javir is by my side.

"You wouldn't wake up," he says gravely.

"She was very tired," Elliz says from where she's mixing together something at a long table on the other side of the tent.

I nod at Javir. "I was. And my leg needed to heal. But I'm fine now."

He looks dubious for a moment but then nods and moves toward Zarix's bed.

"I'm sorry," Javir says simply.

Zarix reaches out and ruffles his hair. "I know. What will you do next time?"

Javir thinks for a moment. "Follow orders."

Zarix nods, and I frown. That's it? That's all they're going to say?

Males. I'll never understand them.

"Can I get up?" I ask Elliz.

She nods and moves toward me. "Gently though. You *must* stay off this leg as it heals."

I nod and reach for my stick. She shakes her head and reaches behind my bed.

My mouth drops open, and I laugh. Crutches. They're wooden without the soft padding, but they're still crutches. Sure, they're a bit medieval-looking compared to those on Earth, but they'll allow me to completely keep weight off my bad leg so it can heal.

"These are amazing, Elliz. Thank you."

She nods, and the smile falls from her face as another healer walks in.

"Zarix must have his wound cleaned," Elliz says softly while Javir talks to Zarix.

"Perhaps..." She gestures at Javir, and I nod. Probably not a good idea for Javir to see Zarix in any more pain. Especially when he already feels responsible.

"I need to find a bathroom," I say. "We should also get something to eat. Will you show me where to go, Javir?"

Zarix's dark gaze meets mine and then flicks to the healer. His expression doesn't change, and I point to the cup on the small table by his bed, gesturing for him to drink it.

He simply raises his eyebrow and points toward the exit.

I reach for my crutches and glower at him as Javir leaves the tent.

"Fine," I tell Zarix. "Deal with the pain. I hope it makes you feel like a man."

He narrows his eyes at me, and then the corner of his mouth tips up, amusement flickering in his eyes.

"You care for me, female," he says softly, and I scowl.

"Learn how to smile properly," I advise him, turning to hobble out of the tent. His soft snort sounds behind me, and I grin.

The camp is huge, and it takes a while for me to get around. Luckily there seems to be a common area close by, and Javir points me toward a row of outhouses.

Whoever cleaned me up has changed me into a long, gauzy dress, and I sigh as I lean my crutches against the wall, balancing on one leg as I haul the material up my legs. I'm exhausted by the time I finish and meet Javir again.

I don't know what was in the cup Elliz gave me, but I'm not drinking any more.

We enter a long tent, and I immediately have flashbacks of my brief stint at summer camp. People are sitting at long tables throughout the tent, chowing down while they talk loudly.

The talking becomes a low murmur when I hobble in and all eyes turn to me.

"Beth," a voice calls, and Javir and I turn as Tazo steps forward.

"Sit down and let me bring you some food," he says. "I'm surprised it wasn't brought to the healers' kradi."

"Zarix needed his wound cleaned," I murmur softly, glancing at Javir, and Tazo nods in understanding.

"Here, sit." The warrior gestures to someone behind me, and a plate is plunked down on the table in front of me.

There's no way I could get through this amount of food in an entire day. The plate has some sort of meat, a few vegetables, and some bread. It's not a huge variety, but the portion sizes...

"Wow."

"Eat," Tazo says, and I smile at him. Javir shovels food in his mouth beside me, and I take a bite.

The meat is tender and juicy, the vegetables crispy, and the bread fresh and still warm. We eat in silence until I finally push my plate away, groaning.

"That was delicious," I say, my eyes widening as I realize how much I just ate. There's still food left on the plate, but I feel so full I could happily curl up and go back to sleep.

"You said there was another human woman here," I say to Tazo, who wipes his mouth as he sits back, taking a gulp from his cup.

He nods and glances up as Perik sits next to us.

Perik raises his eyebrow at me. He turns his head to check that no one is listening and then leans close. "She's a feisty one, that female. Has the qatai in knots."

"Can I see her?"

Perik shrugs. "You'd have to ask the qatai."

I glance at Tazo, who nods. "I'll take you to him."

I reach for my crutches, and he frowns. "I can carry you if you like?"

"Uh. Thanks, but I'm fine. A little exercise is good for me anyway."

And I have no desire to be hauled through the camp like an invalid.

I follow Tazo back through the camp and around the back of the largest tent—the one that seems to sprawl for miles. I know it's not really that big, but after not having seen any large buildings since I was taken from Earth, it seems almost overwhelming in its size.

Two guards are posted at the entrance, but they step aside for Tazo, nodding respectfully. I'm guessing he's pretty high up on the totem pole here.

Tazo holds open the flap of the tent, and I hobble past him, blowing out a breath as I step inside.

"Wow."

The tent looked almost sparse and plain from the outside—a dull beige color. Inside, though, it's almost over-whelming to my senses.

I'm standing in a small room, and my eyes widen as I realize the tent has been sectioned off.

Deep-blue material covers the walls in this section, and thick rugs lie underneath my feet. The heady smell of incense drifts closer, and distantly I can hear the soft strain of music, so quiet it feels almost as if I'm imagining it.

Tazo steps forward, finding a slit in one of the blue sheets of material. This place is like a maze, and it must be an excellent way to prevent any assassination attempts for the qatai. Anyone who managed to make their way in here would then have to successfully navigate the rooms and passageways—one of which we're moving down now.

"Nothing on this planet is what I would expect," I mutter, and Tazo grins at me, his white teeth flashing in the dull light as he turns to the left and pushes open another entrance.

"It's the unexpected that makes life interesting, don't you think?"

"That's one way of looking at it."

The light is brighter here, and I step into a small office. Dexar sits at a desk, and I stare at it as he turns to me. The desk has been carved from a huge block of wood, and it's intricately designed with swirling patterns along the legs and surface.

"Hi," I say stupidly.

"Hello. What do you need?"

I shift. "I heard that there's another human woman here. I was wondering if I could see her?"

If I wasn't watching the qatai closely, I might've missed the frustrated longing that flashes across his face. It's gone an instant later, his expression blank once more as he studies me.

"You may see her. But keep in mind that Alexis will stay here. With me."

His tone is possessive and slightly dark, and I shiver. I can't remember which woman was called Alexis, but whoever she is, I hope the qatai is treating her okay. I've been looked after since the moment we arrived, but the torment in Dexar's eyes concerns me.

"Okay," I say after a long pause. He glances behind me and nods at Tazo, who steps aside for me to leave. I almost laugh. I've just been dismissed.

Tazo leads me deeper into the tent until claustrophobia begins to hit. He glances back and seems to see it on my face because he grins at me.

"There are plenty of exits hidden within this kradi," he says. "It would only take moments before you were outside."

That helps, and I focus on my surroundings, which are getting lusher and lusher as we walk closer to wherever Alexis is being held.

Finally we reach another couple of guards, who nod and open the flap of material.

Alexis turns, and I meet startled ice-blue eyes.

"Oh my God," she says.

"Um, hi."

"Hi? You're the first human woman I've seen for days. Get over here."

I laugh as she strides to me and wraps me in a hug. She pulls back and nods at Tazo, who nods back and leaves us alone.

"You were with the women who were taken during that fight, right?" She shivers as I nod. "Are you with the others? How'd you get in to see me? Tell me everything."

I laugh. This woman looks like a valley girl with her long blonde hair, blue eyes, and tanned skin. But her eyes shine with a keen intelligence, and I won't mistake her exuberance for ditziness.

Her smile drops as I tell her my story. "You haven't heard anything about the other two women taken with you?"

I shake my head. "We were supposed to look for any trace of them when we were in Nexia, but it all went to hell. I didn't keep a good enough eye on the kid—the one traveling with us—and he distracted Zarix. He nearly died, and I was completely focused on getting him back here."

Alexis's eyes turn sympathetic. "That sucks," she says, "but look at the data you do have. We know they're safe. At least they were a few days ago. We know they're with the Voildi, which helps us rule out any other Braxian tribes. And we know the Voildi will likely sell them, based on the way they were talking. That means they're going to have to keep them somewhere. We'll find them."

I blow out a breath. "I needed to hear that. Thanks. How did you end up here anyway?"

Alexis rolls her eyes, gesturing me toward a corner of the room, which is covered in large pillows sprawled on a soft rug. For the first time, I glance around at the large space.

The elegantly draped material on the walls is a deep ruby red, and while I know there are guards outside, it feels like we're in our own little world. The pillows on one side are decorated in gorgeous designs that must take hours of work by hand. On the other side of the room, a large wooden chest stands, two smaller trunks on either side. From the gauzy material hanging out of the larger trunk, I'm guessing that's what passes as Alexis's closet.

Alexis drops gracefully to the floor, perching on one of the larger pillows. She waves her hand toward a collection of wooden bowls filled with fruit and nuts on the small table next to her.

"You hungry?" she asks.

"Wow." I take a seat. "You're living the high life."

She rolls her eyes again. "I am. But it wasn't my first choice, believe me."

I raise an eyebrow, and she fills me in. Apparently, after we were taken, the Braxian warriors who surprised us managed to slaughter the Voildi and took Alexis and three other women back to their tribe.

"Beth," she says seriously, and I meet her eyes. "Did you see what happened to Charlie?"

I cast my mind back, and the memory of my terror in those moments feels like I'm walking on broken glass.

"Charlie? Which one was she?"

"The one with the head wound and all the blood."

"Oh. She wasn't with you guys?"

Alexis shakes her head. "When you were taken, we looked for you, I promise. But the Braxians said we'd have better luck if they came back with more warriors who knew the area and could kill the Voildi. We wanted to find you."

I didn't realize how much I needed to hear those words. Individually, we were nothing to each other—just a bunch of women who all happened to be kidnapped by the Grivath. But we bonded in those few moments where we all came to terms with our fate and tried to find a way to escape.

Something in me relaxes, and I smile at her. "I know. You guys were hurt as well. Now tell me about Charlie."

"She disappeared. We looked everywhere she could have hidden within the area if she was frightened, and we know she wasn't taken with you guys. Nevada, Ellie, and I actually came to this tribe to ask if they'd heard or seen anything."

"What did they say?"

"Well, first, Dexar wouldn't tell us anything until I agreed to stay here with him."

"For how long?"

She glances away. "A year."

"A year?" My voice is high, and I lower it. "Are you kidding me? For a piece of information?"

She meets my eyes and nods. "Yeah. In Dexar's own words, he's a 'bad man.'"

"No shit. Had they seen her?"

"One of his sentries had. And get this: apparently they're convinced she was taken by a dragon."

"A dragon? Get out of here."

Her eyes widen as she nods solemnly, and I take a moment to think it through. There are species on this planet that I could never have imagined on Earth, and I know I've only seen a few. Is it really so hard to believe that dragons exist? Even on Earth, they've been creatures of myth for centuries.

"Okay. Say she has been taken by a dragon. How do we get her back? Do you think it...ate her?"

Alexis's mouth turns down. "I find it strange that she was the only one who was bleeding heavily and she was the one who was taken. I think her blood lured it, and I think it took her for a meal. But the others aren't so sure. So please ask anyone you find about the dragon."

"I will. Wow," I say, still stunned, and then I lean closer. "Are you seriously going to stay here for a year?" I whisper.

She glances at the entrance and brings her head so close that we're almost touching.

"No way," she says. "I'm an astronautical engineer. Not to toot my own horn, but I'm the best hope we have of fixing that ship and getting off this planet."

My mouth drops open, and she lowers her voice so much that I can barely hear her and I'm inches away.

"Nevada and Ellie will come back for me. As soon as we've found the other women, we're all heading back to that ship."

I stare at her for a long moment as it hits me. We could get out of here. I could get back to Earth. Back to my life.

Zarix's hard face flashes before my eyes, and I frown.

Alexis moves away. "What are you thinking?"

"Nothing. I'm excited to get back."

She raises her eyebrow. "That's not the face of someone who's excited."

I sigh. "I am. I want to get back to Earth. You have no idea how much."

"So what's the problem?"

"There's no problem. It's just...Zarix..."

"Ah." She sits back and reaches for a handful of nuts. "A man. Don't they just ruin everything?"

I laugh as she grins at me. "They sure do."

"So what's going on?"

"Nothing, really. It's just...he's the definition of emotionally unavailable, you know? But he kissed me. It was short and sweet and probably the best kiss I've had in my life. How sad is that?"

"It's not sad at all. Girl, maybe you need to tell him how you feel."

My cheeks heat as I imagine him staring at me with those dark eyes. "I don't know how I feel. Plus, he's not really the kind of guy you whisper sweet nothings to."

She rolls her eyes. "So make some kind of move. Life is short. If you get off this planet tomorrow, will you think about what could've been? Will you imagine kissing him?"

I stare at her. "You're a romantic."

She laughs, and the sound is slightly bitter. "I used to be." She glances around at her lush surroundings, and her mouth twists. "I wish I could come help you find the other women," she says softly, and that's the moment that the red cloth parts and Dexar steps inside.

His eyes are hard, and Alexis jumps to her feet.

"What are you doing here?" she asks. "Don't you have minions to be ordering around?"

He glowers at her, no trace of the longing I saw on his face earlier. "Zarix is asking for Beth," he says, and I raise my eyebrow.

Seems fishy to me. Alexis must think the same because her eyes flash as she stares at him.

"What, I'm not allowed to talk to my friends now?"

Dexar looks at me, and I sigh. My bet is that someone has been listening outside and he's pissed at the idea that Alexis is planning to leave his ass.

"I should get back anyway," I say, holding out a hand.

Alexis helps me up and hands me my crutches.

"Come back soon," she says, ignoring Dexar completely, and I give her a hug before making my way out the door.

CHAPTER TEN

Z arix

THE HEALERS' KRADI IS EMPTY WHEN I WAKE AGAIN, AND I
fight the urge to growl. Somehow, over the past few days, I've
become used to the sound of Javir's endless chatter. I've
enjoyed Beth's presence, come to search for her laughing
gaze.

And her lips...

I frown. I don't know what came over me. I know better
than to play with a female. I have nothing to offer her. No
sweet words, no promises of a life together, of children.

It was a mistake.

Perhaps the best mistake of my life, but a mistake all the
same.

I cannot stay here, flat on my back, for a moment longer.
I sit up, testing my muscles, and nod approvingly. Whatever
the healers have done is holding nicely, and while painful, it

is nowhere near the sharp edge of agony that plagued me during the long trip back to camp.

I swing my legs over the side of the bed, taking my time. I do not need to have one of the healers—or worse, Beth—arrive to see me lying on the floor.

My legs hold, and I nod, pleased. I turn as someone steps inside, all pleasure leaving me as Tazo stares at me.

"Should you be on your feet?"

I ignore the question. "Thank you for getting us back to camp. I am in your debt." My last words come out from between gritted teeth, and Tazo snorts. I turn away, finding my shirt and pulling it on.

"What's your plan now, Zarix?"

I tense but force myself to meet his gaze. "I will talk to Dexar and then travel to Tecar's tribe to warn them. Dexar will then decide how many men to send to help."

If one Braxian tribe falls, the repercussions could be enormous for all of us. We must not allow that to happen. We must put the Voildi in the ground. Where they belong.

"And what of the female?" Tazo's voice is slightly amused, and I grind my teeth.

"She will stay here."

I turn away. It's a decision I have only just made. But looking at Tazo, and thinking of the wealth of unsaid words between us...

Tazo snorts. "You believe she will stay where you put her? These human females are not like Braxian females. Ask Dexar if you don't believe me."

"She will have no choice." I reach for my pants, a slight groan leaving me as I bend.

Tazo curses and moves forward, handing them to me. "I never blamed you, you know."

I pull on my pants, gritting my teeth as the movement

tugs at whatever the healers have done to my wound. "I won't talk of this."

Tazo's face is grim as I move past him.

"Eventually you will need to," he says, and I ignore him as I stalk from the kradi.

Dexar's mood is as dark as mine when I meet with him.

"I need some fresh air," he tells me sharply. "Can you walk?"

I narrow my eyes at him, and he sighs, pinching the bridge of his nose. "I did not mean to imply that you were weak," he says, and I nod, following him out of his kradi.

Guards trail us at a distance, but if Dexar even notices them anymore, he doesn't show it.

"I've sent warriors to Rakiz's tribe," he says after we've been walking for a few moments. The sun is hot on my skin, and I gaze up at the sky, Beth's words floating through my head. I can barely imagine a blue sky.

I turn my attention back to Dexar. "If the Voildi have the numbers I fear they do, we will need many warriors from a great number of tribes."

Dexar's mouth thins, and for a moment he looks older than his years.

"Agreed," he says and then glances away, speaking between his teeth. "Alexis believes we are wrong to avoid contact with other tribes."

"Beth has said the same."

"And do you agree?"

I take a moment, and we pause by the river, both of us watching as the water pounds over rocks and stones. Just a few days ago, I would have dismissed the idea. These females are from a different world, where their males have no need to hunt. Beth speaks of something she calls "television," which sounds like sorcery. She talks of camps—cities,

I think she called them—which hold millions of people at once, sprawling into the distance.

And yet perhaps these strange females have a point.

I turn back to Dexar, choosing my words carefully. "Before Gerax's tribe chose to turn on other Braxians, we were becoming open to the idea."

Dexar growls, and I nod, echoing the sentiment. I have not thought of Gerax for some time, but there's little doubt that his actions contributed to the mistrust amongst Braxian tribes.

Not content with the sprawling lands his tribe called home, Gerax wanted more. More of everything. While most tribe kings want nothing more than the health and security of their tribes, Gerax imagined himself as the king of this entire planet.

His tribe attacked, raped, and murdered their way across the face of Agron until we had no choice but to stop them.

Thousands of lives were lost.

Dexar turns, and we begin walking again. "Our trade agreement with Rakiz's tribe began shortly before Gerax inherited his title," he says.

I nod. "And this has been successful for both tribes so far."

"I will think on it," he says. "In the meantime, we must get word to as many tribes as possible. Many will not believe us, but our messengers must convey that without joining to help protect Tecar's tribe, they may fall to the Voildi next."

I shake my head at the thought. "Who could have imagined that the Voildi would be an actual threat to Braxian tribes?"

Dexar growls. "We live in confusing times."

"I need to ask for a favor."

"What do you need?"

"Javir, the boy. Someone needs to take him back to his mother."

Dexar raises an eyebrow, amusement clear on his face for the first time since we left his kradi. "And I suppose this someone will not be you."

I shake my head. "I will go directly to Tecar's tribe. I will leave the boy and the female here."

Dexar's amusement deepens, and I scowl as he smiles.

"You believe this is a good idea?"

I ignore the pang of guilt at leaving Beth behind, the strange longing I feel when she is not near. Instead, I think of how close she came to death in the tavern.

I nod to Dexar, turning back toward camp. "I do."

Beth

The music sounds, and I'm dancing, arms fluttering up and down in the illusion of flight.

"Arabesque! Point those feet! Good, now plié." Miss Jay is demanding, but a simple approving nod from her is worth more than glowing praise from any other dance teacher.

I sink into a plié, feeling my body stretch. Then I'm twirling, pausing briefly with my arms raised in the air. I jump into an entrechat six, beating my feet together as I leap as high as possible.

"Now get high for that grand jeté," Miss Jay says, and I leap across the studio, both legs lifting into the air until they're parallel with the ground.

My leg hurts as I point my feet, and I jolt awake, staring down at my leg. The worst thing about being injured on this planet? There are no X-rays, MRIs, or ultrasounds.

I have no idea how badly I'm really hurt.

I've been dancing since I was three years old. Of course, at that age, I wasn't truly dancing, but I loved it. My parents wanted me to try a range of hobbies and interests when I was a kid, but I always went back to ballet. I adored the music, the costumes, the way the ballerinas would float across the stage. When I finally began performing, I was hooked.

I sigh. Thinking about it is just making me depressed.

I glance over at Zarix's bed and freeze.

It's empty.

It wasn't empty when we went to sleep last night. In fact, Zarix looked at me for a long moment, his gaze searching my face as if he was memorizing it. Finally he gave me a gruff "good night" and closed his eyes.

I can tell by the darkness in the tent that it's still early. Javir's soft snores sound, and I sit up slowly, careful not to wake him.

My crossbow is lying on Zarix's bed. Someone has carefully cleaned it, and the canvas bag of bolts sits beside it.

The bastard has left me.

The feeling sinks into me with the same kind of certainty I felt when the Voildi lifted me and carried me out of that clearing.

Panic flutters in my chest, and I swing my legs over the bed. I pull on one of the gauzy dresses Alexis left for me and reach for my crutches. Then I run my hand over Zarix's bed and turn for the door.

His blankets are still warm.

He thinks he can leave me behind like a puppy he changed his mind about adopting?

Game. On.

I gasp with exertion as I swing my leg, the wooden

crutches digging into my skin as I haul myself through the camp. I've seen where the mishua are kept, in a large, guarded area close to the camp entrance.

I'm out of breath, but I make it. Zarix is standing by his mishua, packing provisions into saddlebags.

"You son of a bitch!" I shout, panting as I force myself to move faster. "You were seriously going to leave me here?"

Zarix's face is completely blank, and that just pisses me off more. He watches me approach, and Rexi snorts as I get close.

"Yeah, fuck you too," I tell her and then turn back to Zarix. "What is wrong with you? Haven't you ever heard the definition of 'teamwork'?"

A muscle beats in his jaw as his dark eyes bore into mine. "I'm going to Tecar's tribe," he finally grits out. "It's too dangerous for you."

"Too dangerous for you, you mean. Admit it—you're scared I'll almost get you killed again."

My voice is bitter, and his eyes widen slightly. "Is that what you think?" he asks.

I wave my hand. "Regardless, we had a deal. I still have no information about Ivy and Zoey. You know how important it is that I find them."

"Is that all this is about?" he asks, his gaze suddenly intent. "The other human women?"

I glower at him. "What else could it possibly be about?"

He lets out a rough curse, and I yelp as he takes a step closer, buries his hand in my hair, and crashes his mouth into mine.

All thought flees my brain.

His mouth is hard and hot, and my thoughts grind to a halt as a lightning bolt of desire flashes through my body.

I slide my hands under his shirt, fingers playing over the

bumps of his abs. He shudders, and then he's pulling away, his face fierce as he glares down at me.

"You make me insane," he growls, and a breathless laugh leaves my mouth.

"Ditto."

His brow lowers, and then I squeak as he leans down, lifting me until I twine my legs around his hips. He grabs my crutches in one hand and then he's striding back toward our kradi.

"Where are we going?"

"We're going to finish this," he says, and I narrow my eyes on his face. His jaw is hard, eyes flinty as he stalks down the path between the kradis.

Oh no, my grumpy warrior. We're just getting started.

It's as if he heard my thoughts because his eyes meet mine, his growing hotter as we reach the kradi. I expect him to let me go, but he simply ducks his head, holding me close as he steps inside and drops my crutches on the floor.

Zarix sits on the furs, taking care not to bump my calf.

He pulls at the string at the front of the dress, and then he freezes, a muscle ticking in his jaw as he stares down at me.

I look down and blush. My breasts are small, but the cut of the dress has created cleavage where there is usually none. My boobs are popping out of my dress, framed by the gauzy material. I raise my hands to cover them, and Zarix shakes his head, pulling the dress over my shoulders, trapping my arms by my side.

"Hey!"

He ignores that, and then his mouth gets busy as he leans down, running his lips along the tops of my breasts. I gasp, ridiculously turned on, and he glances up at me, watching my face as he pulls my dress down lower and moves his mouth to my nipple.

My thighs clench as he laves it, caressing, playing, and slowly driving me out of my mind.

"Zarix," I moan, but he simply continues, taking his own sweet time.

"And you think *I* make *you* crazy?" I say, and he meets my gaze, the look in his eyes wicked. I move my hips until he's aligned against me, the thick length of his cock right where I need it. I rub against him, and his eyes darken as his hands tighten on my arms.

Two can play at this game.

He raises his head and takes my mouth again, his tongue sliding past my lips, erasing the memory of any man who kissed me in the past.

I sigh into our kiss, still unable to believe that this might finally happen.

Zarix pushes the dress up my thighs, sliding his hand down to gently play with the damp, sensitive heat of my sex.

Pleasure runs up my spine, leaving me gasping as he finds my clit. I moan, and he swallows the sound, continuing to claim me with his mouth.

I tremble, flooding his hand, and he slowly draws his head back, staring at me, his cheekbones flushed with arousal.

I clutch his shoulders, my nails digging in as he continues to watch me steadily. I'd think he was unaffected if not for the blazing heat of his gaze and the almost pained look on his face as he clamps his teeth together.

I reach down and find his cock, butterflies playing in my stomach at the size of him.

"Will you even fit?" I whisper, and humor lights his eyes.

"I will. I promise."

I'm nervous, but the idea of him inside me, filling me up...

He brushes his finger over my clit again, and I grind against him, on the edge.

"Inside me," I gasp, and he slowly shakes his head, his gaze on my face.

He slides a finger inside me, twisting it until he finds *that* spot, and I break out in a sweat, groaning. His thumb plays with my clit while his finger steadily thrusts, and I grind against him as his hard mouth finds mine. He fucks my mouth with his tongue as he strokes me with his fingers, and I whine, on the edge of something incredible.

I almost scream as my body explodes, pleasure peaking as I arch against him, moaning as my hips twitch uncontrollably.

He groans against my mouth, and then I'm blinking up at him as he lays me gently on my back.

Within moments he's naked, and I help him pull my dress over my head. His skin is warm and smooth, and my fingers dance over his chest. His scales glimmer, and I trace them, fascinated, but Zarix is already finding my mouth again as he gently pulls my thighs apart, sliding his cock inside me.

He goes slow, allowing me to get used to the size of him. There's a moment of discomfort as my body stretches around him, but he slides his hand down, once again finding my clit. The brush of his finger along my sensitive nub makes me arch against him. He slides further inside me until his pelvis is hard against mine, and then he's filling me up in a way I hadn't thought possible.

He slides his arm under my hips and pulls his head back, his dark gaze meeting mine as he thrusts. I gasp, and his eyes light with something like triumph as he pulls back, thrusting again.

Oh God. An orgasm is positioned on the horizon, just out of reach, and I know instinctively that it will destroy me. It's almost frightening, and I slam my eyes closed, twisting my hips away.

"Oh, no you don't."

Zarix's low voice is amused, and I open my eyes to find him smiling at me even as his whole body shakes with the effort of holding back.

He leans down, taking my nipple in his mouth again. My breath catches in my throat as he grazes it with the edge of his teeth, and he does it again, twisting his hips and grinding against my clit as he thrusts deep.

I explode.

He slams his mouth down on mine, muffling my loud cry as every muscle in my body shakes and my vision dims. My orgasm is so powerful it's almost scary, and it goes on and on as Zarix continues to thrust, drawing out my pleasure. Finally he stills against me, a low groan leaving his throat as he climaxes.

We're silent for a long moment, panting and shaking. Then Zarix rolls off me, hauling me close to him, and I stare at the ceiling of the tent, stunned.

So that's what great sex is like.

I've had mediocre sex before. I've even had good sex. But Zarix puts the same dedication and focus into lovemaking as he puts into everything else. And the results? Amazing.

We lie silent for a long time, and my eyes are heavy when Zarix stirs and runs his hand over my hair. I crack open my eyes and find him staring down at me.

Often when Zarix looks at me, it's as if he's slightly

confused. As if he doesn't quite know what to do with me. I smile at him, and his frown deepens.

"What's up?" I ask.

"I don't fully understand how this happened," he says, and I feel my smile widen.

"If you need me to explain the birds and the bees, I can," I murmur.

"The birds and the bees?" The confusion on his face is somehow ridiculously cute, and I crawl my way up his body and nibble at his lips.

"Here's a hint," I say, running my hand down his chest. "You're tab *A*, and I'm slot *B*."

Zarix stares up at me for a moment, and then my heart stops as a slow, wicked grin spreads across his face.

"Oh God," I groan, burying my head in his chest. "You shouldn't have done that."

I peek up at him, and thankfully his smile is gone. His eyes are still lit with amusement though, and I feel my heart give one hard thump. The relaxed, slightly bewildered yet delighted expression is one I want to see from him every day.

"I thought you wanted me to smile," he says. He wraps his hand in my hair and guides my face back up to his for another kiss.

I grin against his lips. "Caveman."

Zarix looks at me for a few more seconds, and I see the moment he shuts down. His face goes blank again, and he releases his hold on my hair, shifting his gaze to the roof of the tent.

The sudden change stings, and I pull back.

"Will you tell me about it?" I ask softly, and his gaze whips to mine.

"What do you know?" he demands, and I blow out a breath, choosing to ignore his tone.

"I know that whoever made you avoid people the way you do, whoever made you so afraid of caring about anyone, must have been an incredible person."

He nods, looking away, but his arm shifts down to pull me close again. "She was. Hana was light and laughter. She never met anyone she couldn't make smile. She would do anything to cheer someone up if they weren't happy. It was what she lived for."

I ignore the stab of jealousy that jolts through my chest. I refuse to feel envious of a dead woman. And she must be dead because I can't imagine anything else causing the complete shutdown of a man as virile as Zarix.

"She was Tazo's sister," he says softly.

Wow. That explains some of the history those two must have.

"What happened?"

"She believed we would one day be mates. I told her many times that this wasn't the case. We were friends. From the moment she could walk, she'd followed Tazo and me from place to place. I saw her almost as a sister myself."

I wince. "You told her that?"

He gives me an affronted look. "Of course not. But I made it clear that I had no intention of being her mate. I would have been her friend until the end of my days," he says softly, pain stark in his voice, and I reach up to run my fingers through his hair.

"She didn't like hearing that," I guess.

He shakes his head, shifting so I can reach more of his hair.

"She was young, beautiful, and kind in a tribe that was

becoming almost desperate for females. She could have chosen any male she liked."

"But she wanted you," I say, and he nods, his brow lowering and confusion clear on his face.

"On that last day, I snapped at her. I told her it would never happen and to go and play with a male who had time for her." Self-loathing is clear in his voice, and I reach down to stroke my finger along his clenched fist.

"She knew you didn't mean it," I say. "The woman you're describing would have forgiven you. You know that, right?"

He shrugs. "I left on a hunting trip. I hadn't known, but she decided to follow me. I had already been gone for many hours and never knew. She was found by the Voildi. They left only her head behind."

"Oh my God. I'm so sorry, Zarix."

He nods, his gaze still on the roof. "It was my job to protect her that day. Tazo put his trust in me, and I failed."

I sigh. "She was responsible for her own decisions. You know that, right?"

He's silent, and I study the stubborn line of his jaw. To a man like Zarix, who is obviously the protective type, her death would have proved that he was incapable of looking after the people he cared about.

I get it now. Why he didn't want to take me with him, why he was so mad when Javir appeared, and why he's constantly so snarly. He doesn't want to be responsible for our safety.

And then I went and ran after him when he tried to leave—the same way Hana did on that terrible day.

I lay my head back on Zarix's chest, and he moves his hand to my hair, stroking it.

"So soft," he rumbles, and I smile.

Somehow I've managed to catch feelings for this bad-tempered, overprotective male. Feelings that I'm damn sure he has no intention of ever returning.

I wish I could talk to my mom. She'd tell me exactly what I need to hear in this situation. For a moment, I miss my parents so much that I could curl up and cry. Nothing was ever the same after they were killed by a drunk driver a few years ago.

Zarix sighs. "I must go."

I lift my head, narrowing my eyes at him. "*We* must go. Don't think you're leaving me behind, buster. I promise I won't get in the way...more than absolutely necessary," I finish as he gives me a look.

He heaves a sigh but sits up, and I study the way his abs flex and roll, attempting to ignore the bandage at his side.

"Fine, female," he growls, and I grin. "I am obviously helpless to your...charms."

I laugh, ridiculously pleased at his teasing. The rough, surly warrior is sexy as hell, but the open, relaxed male is the one who intrigues me the most.

I pull on my clothes, and Zarix scowls as I reach for my pants, leaning down so he can put them on me himself.

"How is your leg?" he asks, voice gentle.

"It's getting better," I say. "The crutches help."

He nods and hands them to me, and then we make our way out of the kradi. The sun has now risen, and I follow Zarix back to his mishua.

Javir waits for us, my crossbow swinging from one hand, his knife clutched in the other.

Zarix curses in Braxian, my translator not quite picking it up. I only know it's a bad word because Javir's eyes widen before a grin crosses his face.

I glance at Zarix. "We should probably try not to swear in front of the kid," I mutter, and Javir rolls his eyes, giving us a look that says we're the two dumbest people he knows.

"You were going to leave without me," he says, his blue face scrunched up in indignation.

Zarix studies him, and I can practically see him calling the kid a pain in the ass in his head.

I nudge him in the ribs with my elbow, and he meets my gaze.

"Are we going anywhere near his mom's house?" I ask. "She must be worried sick."

Zarix's expression looks like he swallowed something nasty, but he finally nods, gesturing for the mishua.

Javir scrambles up on it, and I study the other mishua in the pen, who are currently being fed by one of the warriors.

"Beth."

I turn at Alexis's voice and raise my eyebrow. In this camp of warriors, she sticks out like a sore thumb. Her white-blonde hair hangs down her back like a silk sheet, and she's dressed in a long, gauzy blue gown that matches her eyes.

"Oh, hey," I say.

Alexis runs her eyes over my hair and grins at me. From the look on her face, I have sex hair. I blush, and she laughs while Zarix turns, deftly grabbing the knife out of Javir's hand.

Tuning them out as they begin to bicker, I move closer to Alexis as she hands me a large canvas bag.

"I thought you could use some more clothes," she says. "I packed some more food in there as well."

"That's so thoughtful. Thanks."

She just bites her lip, her face suddenly serious. "I wish I could come help."

I glance behind her to where Dexar stands, his face blank as he watches us.

"You've got your work cut out for you here," I tease, and she glances at Dexar and then gives me a look.

"Travel safe," she says, throwing her arms around me, squeezing tight.

"We will. Thanks." I hug her back and then turn to Zarix, who takes my crutches, handing them to Javir. Then he lifts me onto the mishua and hauls himself up behind me, and we plod away from the camp.

CHAPTER ELEVEN

Z arix

THE DAY IS LONG, BUT I PASS THE TIME BY ENJOYING THE SWEET smell of Beth's hair. She laughs at something Javir says, and I feel my mouth twitch at the musical sound.

We camp on the outskirts of the Seinex Forest, and I cook the udazin I hunted on our way. I hand Beth one of the choicest parts, and she takes a bite.

"Mmm," she says. "Tastes like chicken."

I don't know what chicken is, but this is obviously a good thing given Beth's enjoyment of the meat.

Javir grins at me from across the fire. We will need to put out the flames soon. Otherwise, we risk drawing predators.

The thought of Beth in danger makes my heart race, and I glance at the boy. He is young, with his whole life ahead of him. His mother would never forgive me if I let him die.

"What are you thinking?" Beth asks.

I hand her another piece of meat, and she chews with obvious relish.

"I'm thinking that you need to eat more," I say, and she gives me a look.

"That's not what you were thinking," she mutters but glances away, effectively ending our conversation.

I jump to my feet, drawing my sword, and Beth pales, the meat falling from her hand.

"Someone comes," I murmur, glancing at Javir. He pulls his knife, and I narrow my eyes at him. The boy has skills. Once again, I did not feel him take it from me.

Javir moves in front of Beth, and she heaves an exasperated sigh. I ignore them and move from the fire, eyes focused, body ready.

"Relax, Zarix," a deep voice says, and I curse as Tazo steps out from behind a tree.

"What are you doing here?" I growl.

Tazo's gaze flicks behind me, and I turn, watching as Beth lets out a sigh of relief, sitting back on the overturned tree and resuming her meal.

"Dexar sent me with you. You left earlier than I had anticipated."

"I don't need your help," I growl.

He laughs, although his eyes are hard. "Regardless, you have it." He gestures, and Dekir and Perik join him.

I curse and turn back to the fire. Beth sends me a sympathetic look while Javir moves to the warriors, immediately chatting about the journey.

I ignore them as they join us, cooking their own beast. Tazo offers Beth a piece of meat, and I tamp down my jealousy when she takes it, giving him one of her sweet smiles in return.

I work best alone. But once I process the fact that Dexar

chose not to tell me he was sending these warriors with me, I will likely feel gratitude for their presence. The more warriors with us, the more swords between any Voildi and the female and child.

Perik puts out the fire, and I move to my furs. Beth picks up her own furs, dragging them close to mine, and I avoid Tazo's gaze as I lie down, hauling her close to me.

I should tell Beth to move her furs away, but I can't control my instinct to keep her near me.

She lets out a pleased hum, and I grit my teeth as I instantly harden. Out the corner of my eye, I can see the other warriors setting up camp in various locations around the small clearing, closer to the trees.

Beth instantly falls asleep with her head on my shoulder, and I stroke her hair as I stare up at the stars. It's strange to imagine how different the night sky must look on her planet.

Truthfully, everything about this delicate female is different. But despite our differences, we fit. Beth's voice echoes in my head, teasing me about tab *A* and slot *B*, and in spite of my mood, I fall asleep with a smile on my face.

***

Beth

I wake gasping, and a hard mouth slams down on mine, swallowing my moan.

"Shh," Zarix says, and I gulp down air as his clever fingers stroke and play. I twist my head, but the others are still snoring, spaced out around the clearing, and the sun hasn't yet risen.

Zarix's other hand is almost desperate. I slept in one of

his shirts last night, and he pushes it up over my thighs, undoing the front tie with his mouth.

He uses his chin to push open the shirt until my breasts are bared. Then the calloused skin of his palm scratches across my nipple, and I gasp again as I lift my hips, urging him on. His fingers slide through the slippery heat of me, and then he lowers his mouth again, capturing my moan as I arch against him, shaking with pleasure.

I gulp at the air as he releases my mouth, and the rest of the world falls away as he thrusts inside me. Nothing else matters except the thick heat of him as he moves smoothly into a hard rhythm, his hands sliding under my hips.

He shifts his angle, letting out a low, strained laugh as he grinds against my clit, and I slap my own hand over my mouth. His eyes light, shining with both lust and amusement, and my legs shake before everything breaks apart, pleasure ripping through my body with the force of a tsunami. Zarix shudders, an almost noiseless growl leaving his throat.

We stay like this for a long moment, both of us panting. Then Zarix pulls me close until I'm lying slumped on his chest. He strokes my back as my breathing slows. He's out of breath too, still shuddering as we both come down. I don't know what his orgasm was like, but if it was anything like mine...

He slides his hand over my butt, and I lift my head, grinning at him.

"I'm surprised you want me this way," I joke, but a tiny, insecure part of me is all too serious. "I'm too thin, remember?"

Zarix frowns. "I didn't mean to insult you, Beth. From the moment I saw you lying in that trap, I wanted you. And the thought of you not having enough food...it made me crazed."

I tilt my head. "Is that why you're constantly feeding me?"

At every turn, he's attempting to shove food in my mouth.

He nods. "You are beautiful, and I would not change one thing about you. But on this planet, we eat well during the good times so that we are prepared for lean times."

I nod. I guess I get it. Braxians are much larger than humans, so most of us must seem puny in comparison, and given that I've been watching what I put in my mouth since I was a teenager, it makes sense that he would worry.

We lie in silence for a long moment, and I practically purr as he strokes my hair.

"Tell me about your dance," he says.

I smile up at him. "It's okay," I say. "We can talk about something else."

He frowns. "I want to understand you."

I don't even know where to start, but I take a deep breath.

"From the moment I saw a performance of *The Nutcracker* on TV, I knew I wanted to be a ballerina. When it turned out I had some natural talent, I convinced my parents to let me homeschool so I could have more lessons. And when I got the chance to go away to a dance-focused boarding school, I did that too."

"What is a boarding school?"

"Um. You know how the children in your tribe have lessons?"

He nods, and I realize this idea must seem crazy to someone who grew up in a tribe that, while huge, seems to be a tight-knit community.

"Well," I continue, "this is kind of like that, only my boarding school was days and days of travel away if you were to be traveling by mishua. I saw my parents a couple of times a month."

"You must have missed them," Zarix says.

I nod. "Yeah. But I wanted to be the best. My dream was to be a prima ballerina. I danced in the corps for three years before I got my chance. The day after we were kidnapped by the Grivath was the day I was supposed to dance as the Swan Queen in *Swan Lake*. I've danced the role before, but every time is different. Every time is a new challenge." I let my voice trail off, and then I say it. The sentence I haven't let myself think, even in my head.

"This might have been my last season with the New York City Ballet," I say quietly. "It's not uncommon for injuries to force us into retirement." I let my voice trail off and lay my head back on his chest, soaking in the reality of my life.

When a dancer retires from ballet, they're usually less than thirty years old, without any savings, often injured, and with no college degree because they ignored school in favor of dancing. I have more savings than most because I was lucky enough to teach in the off season when I was in the corps. But retiring means coming up with a whole new life. A life I was never prepared for.

And the injury? I look down at my bandaged left leg, and a bitter laugh escapes me.

"You know, this leg has been plaguing me for years. I snapped a tendon when I was in the corps, and a year ago, I ruptured my Achilles."

My stomach clenches, and I feel a cool sweat break out on the back of my neck at the memory of the *pop* that sounded like a gunshot as I fell on stage. After surgery and almost a year of grueling physical therapy, I was finally ready to return to the stage.

I sigh. "I guess I should be thankful it's the same leg, huh?"

Zarix is silent for a moment, and I smile sadly. I know he doesn't understand most of what I'm talking about, but it helps to say what I've lost out loud.

"I'm sorry," Zarix says softly. "You are a strong, resilient female."

I smile. Despite Zarix's gruff exterior, he somehow knows exactly what I need to hear.

"Thanks," I say.

"What of your family?"

"I'm an only child. Which was lucky 'cause ballet is expensive, and I don't think my parents could have afforded to pay for if they'd had any more kids."

I move up Zarix's body, burying my face in his neck as I swallow around the lump in my throat.

"My parents were hit by a drunk driver a few years ago. I wonder if I'd known then what I know now—that everything I worked for would disappear—if I would've stayed home. I could've spent more time with them, time that I'll never get to have now that they're gone."

Zarix is silent, running his hand up and down my back. Before I know it, I'm bawling, sniffling as quietly as I can while he pulls me close, letting me wet his neck with my tears.

I feel strangely...empty. Am I going through the stages of grief? Is the low-level depression that has been plaguing me just my brain's way of attempting to accept the inevitable?

I push that thought away.

"What about your parents?" I ask.

"My mother died when I was a child. She was attacked

by a wild animal, and the healers were unable to fix the damage. My father...left."

"What do you mean, he left?"

Zarix's chest lifts my head slightly as he shrugs. "One day I woke up, and he was gone. He left the tribe. I was raised by my mother's sister."

"I'm so sorry, Zarix."

He strokes my hair again, one of his fingers brushing my ear, and I shiver. He pauses as if noting my reaction and runs his finger along the same spot.

My thighs clench, and I raise my head, meeting his wicked gaze.

"I'm hungry," Javir announces, sitting up across the clearing. Zarix adjusts our clothes under the blanket, a look of such disappointment on his face that I can't help but laugh.

"Later," I promise him, shivering as I roll out of our warm nest, reach for my crutches, and get to my feet.

Beth

"It's...gone," I murmur.

We've been traveling for hours, and now Javir's howl echoes through the forest as he jumps off the mishua.

We all stare at the empty spot where his home used to be.

There's nothing left.

"Voildi," Zarix growls behind me, shaking with tension. "I can still smell them."

He jumps down and helps me off Rexi, handing me my crutches.

Javir falls to his knees. "Mother?"

His voice is small, and my chest tightens.

"Why would they do this?" I ask.

Zarix stares at the black wreckage of Sonis's and Javir's lives, his gaze hard. "It was known that Javir and his mother were under Braxian protection. Under *my* protection. This is a message."

"Do you think..." I don't finish the sentence as Javir makes a tiny, broken sound. The other warriors dismount, growls leaving their throats as they take in the sight.

"I don't know," Zarix says softly. "If they took his mother, they would have left us a sign."

I swallow down bile. "A sign" like her head. Arguably, burning her house to the ground was a sign, but what do I know?

Javir gets to his feet and, without looking at any of us, runs into the forest.

"Shit," I mutter.

Zarix moves to go after him, and I grab his elbow.

"Let me." He hesitates, and I sigh. "He worships you, Zarix. He won't want you to see him fall apart."

Zarix stares after Javir for a moment and then finally nods. I slowly make my way after Javir, giving him a few minutes alone.

I find him slumped on the ground, curled against a tree. Tears roll down his face as he stares into the forest, and I drop my crutches and sit down next to him.

I forget sometimes that Javir is just a kid. And right now, he's a kid who wants his mother.

I still want mine, and I'm twenty-seven.

I wrap my arm around him, and he turns, burying his face in my chest as a sob rips from his body.

"It's going to be okay," I whisper, stroking his dark hair

off his blue face. I rock him, letting him cry it out, and we spend long minutes on the forest floor, resting against a bone-white tree.

Finally he pulls away from me, his gaze blank. "I'm going to kill them all," he says.

"Javir, listen to me. I said listen." I shake his shoulders until he focuses on my face. "We don't know what happened to her. Does your mom ever leave the house? Maybe she went for a walk. She could have met a friend. Don't have her dead and buried when she could be out there, just as worried about you."

He sniffs, wiping his face with the back of his hand. "If they killed her, it's all my fault," he bites out. "I shouldn't have left."

Zarix's deep voice sounds, and I turn my head.

"If you'd stayed, you might have been in the tashiv when they set it on fire," he says. Zarix crouches next to us, his gaze intent. "I'll help you find out what happened," he says, and Javir nods, wiping the last of the tears from his face.

He clears his throat, obviously embarrassed, and gets to his feet. "And then we'll make them pay."

Zarix nods, standing and helping me up. "Yes. We'll make them pay. I promise."

Javir's expression is still crestfallen, and Zarix pulls him into a fierce hug. My heart melts at the sight, and I wipe tears off my cheeks before picking up my crutches.

Zarix pulls away and wipes a tear off Javir's face. Javir's cheeks turn a darker shade of blue, and Zarix frowns.

"It's okay to cry," he says. "Now let's go."

We're a solemn group as we get back on our mishua. The other warriors are quiet over the next few hours until Zarix tenses behind me.

"Voildi," he says in a low hiss, exchanging a look with Tazo. He jumps off the mishua, glancing at me.

"Stay here."

I nod, and Tazo gestures to Perik, who dismounts, moving with Zarix.

A branch snaps under Perik's foot, and he grimaces as Zarix turns his head, sending him an icy look.

We're all tense, and Javir looks at me wide-eyed as we wait for them to return.

Moments later, my mouth drops open as Zarix appears, his huge arm wrapped tightly around the neck of a struggling Voildi. The light-yellow skin of the Voildi's face has darkened as he fights for air, and Javir's eyes light with savage pleasure as Zarix drags the Voildi close to us.

The other warriors jump off their mishua and make quick work of gagging the Voildi and tying him to Perik's mishua. Then Zarix pulls himself up onto our mishua, wrapping his arm around my middle and holding tight as he gestures to the others, and we move.

We don't waste time.

I open my mouth, still stunned as Rexi picks up the pace.

"What—"

"Shh," Zarix murmurs in my ear. "By now, the Voildi will know that one of their own has been taken. We must move quickly."

I nod, and we ride for what seems like hours until Zarix and the others are sure that we're not being followed. Then we find a small clearing and dismount, and I watch as Tazo pulls the Voildi off the mishua, letting him fall to the ground.

Then they take off his gag. Zarix pulls a knife, holding it in front of the Voildi's face.

"Go ahead and scream," he says, holding the knife up until the sun glints off the sharp blade.

The Voildi thins his lips but says nothing, and Perik looks away as if he can't bear to watch.

I frown, but my attention is drawn straight back to the Voildi as Zarix begins questioning him.

"Who burned the tashiv?"

"Which tashiv?"

Zarix runs his knife along the Voildi's yellow neck, and my stomach clenches as blood appears.

"Killis's pack," the Voildi says. "He said it was retaliation from when you wiped out Gito's pack."

Javir steps forward. "That pack killed my father."

Zarix frowns over his shoulder at Javir, but the Voildi seems to get more nervous as he stares at Javir even as his lips thin.

"Where's my mother?" Javir demands, and Zarix sighs but hits the Voildi in the face when he stays silent.

"Answer him."

"I don't know. The Krinir wasn't there," the Voildi spits out, and Javir turns away, his face falling slack with relief.

Zarix told me that Javir's race are called the Krinir, which means Javir's mom is safe.

"Females," Zarix says, gesturing toward me. "Like her. Where are they?"

The Voildi says nothing, and I have to turn away as Zarix cuts him again. The Voildi's scream is quickly cut off.

I turn back, attempting to ignore the blood dripping down the Voildi's face.

"Malufic," he chokes out when Zarix removes his hand. "They're in Malufic while Killis finds buyers for them."

I grit my teeth so hard I worry that they might crack, and

any sympathy I have for the bruised and bleeding Voildi disappears in a rush.

The Voildi are a blight on this planet. They kidnap women and sell them. They burn people's homes to the ground. They're planning to attack Braxian tribes.

Oh, and they *eat* people.

"Tell me everything about the attack on Tecar's tribe," Zarix says, and the Voildi is silent.

Tazo lets out a low laugh. "That's right," he says. "We know all about your plans. Tell us what we want to know, and we'll let you go."

Zarix glances at me, gesturing toward Javir with his head. I shake mine, and he narrows his eyes at me, sending me a look.

I sigh. He obviously doesn't want me around for this, and truthfully, my stomach is probably too weak for it anyway. I move to Javir, who glares at me, his face pale, but finally follows me to the opposite side of the clearing as the Braxians' voices drop to low murmurs.

It only takes a few more minutes, and then Javir tenses, vibrating with fury beside me.

"What?" Javir's voice cracks with outrage.

I turn, and we both watch as Zarix prowls toward us.

"You're letting him go?" Javir growls, indignant, and my mouth drops open as Perik cuts the rope around the Voildi's ankles and wrists. The Voildi doesn't hesitate, his face and neck bright with blood as he hauls ass out of the clearing.

"Why would you do that?" I ask, and Zarix keeps his eyes on Javir.

"Voildi are nothing without their pack," he says softly. "They are unable to hunt alone."

I consider this. Voildi sound similar to the way hyenas

are depicted on Earth—as brutal scavengers who will eat anything and hunt together until their prey is worn out.

Javir is still glowering at Zarix, who sighs, turning to scan the clearing.

"The Voildi will know he has been captured and tortured. Since they are cowards, they'll also know he told us valuable information. If he returns to his pack, they will kill him."

Javir thinks for a moment and then finally nods, and I get it. Zarix has given the Voildi a fate worse than death.

"I'll ride with Tazo," Javir says, walking away.

Zarix turns to me, his expression blank, and gestures toward the mishua. "Let's go."

I follow him, but he barely looks at me as he helps me mount.

"What's wrong?" I ask.

He's silent for a long moment as we continue on our journey.

Finally he speaks, leaning close as he murmurs in my ear. "The Voildi revealed that a Braxian tribe has agreed to work with them to attack Tecar's tribe."

My mouth drops open. "No way."

I feel him nod and turn my head, almost flinching at the rage on his face. For Braxians to betray their people this way...

I frown. "Why would they do it?"

A muscle jumps in his jaw, and he focuses on the back of Javir's head as the mishua in front of us flicks out her back leg, discouraging Rexi from getting too close.

Rexi snorts and lowers her head, her horns gleaming in the sun.

Zarix lets out one low growl, and the mishua go back to ignoring each other.

"Because their territory has decreased in size," he bites out finally. "Lafa, their king, has more ego than competence and has allowed his warriors to become soft. Now they hope to capitalize on Tecar's loss, splitting his territory with the Voildi."

I grimace. *Wow.* These warriors have a strong code of honor, and from the grim silence of our group, it's clear that the Braxians are going to make Lafa hurt real bad before they kill him.

CHAPTER TWELVE

Z arix

"Put down your weapons," I growl, jumping off the mishua. "We come with news for Tecar. It's urgent."

It's easy to see why this tribe will be the first targeted by the Voildi. And if Lafa truly believes that the Voildi will share this territory with him, he's stupider than I had imagined.

His tribe would be next. And the Voildi would continue to join together, waging war across this planet.

We were practically at the camp gates before the sentries surrounded us. If we were the Voildi attacking this tribe, we would already have the upper hand.

"State your business." This Braxian is grizzled, but he carries no extra weight around his middle, and his gaze is clear and direct as he finally releases his hold on his sword.

Beth lets out a shaky breath behind me, and I attempt to push down the rage at the threat to my female.

My *female?*

I push the thought away and wait while the sentries decide whether to allow us entry. Tazo glances at me, and I shake my head. While I have little doubt that the four of us could take down these sentries, it would simply guarantee that Tecar would see us as a threat.

Plus, there is a chance that Beth or Javir could be injured.

Instead, I reach for patience and wait while one of the sentries moves back toward camp to notify Tecar of our visit.

It is the king himself who meets us at the camp entrance, a fact that has his guards tense and ready.

"If you are from Dexar's tribe, then you know better than to arrive with no warning," he says, his gaze scanning me before resting on Beth for a long moment.

"I apologize," I say formally. "But this is a matter of grave importance."

Tecar is no longer the young male I remember from my own youth. Now he has grown into his role, and his expression is carefully guarded as he finally nods and waves a hand at his guards. "Let them in."

I pull myself back onto the mishua, ignoring the sharp pain as the movement pulls at the wound in my side.

The camp is silent as we move through it, and I automatically note weaknesses in Tecar's defenses.

Tecar doesn't miss this, but he simply raises his eyebrow as if unconcerned, leading us toward his kradi. Servants step forward to take our mishua, and a group of children laugh as they throw stones on the ground, jumping around them in a game known only to them.

Beth watches the children and meets my eyes. I nod. If the Voildi are successful, this will all be gone. We *must* make Tecar listen.

Tecar steps into his kradi, followed by his guards. Tazo follows, and I gesture for Beth and Javir to walk between us while Perik and Dekir bring up the rear.

Tecar gestures for us to take a seat. The air has turned cooler, and I guide Beth to a spot by the fire, taking her crutches from her. She smiles up at me, and I feel the sudden urge to take her mouth, to claim her in front of all these males.

I grind my teeth and hand Dekir the crutches instead, waiting for Tecar to sit. He immediately scans us again, his gaze piercing.

"Tell me," he growls, and I clamp down my irritation at the order. "Please," he says, likely noting my reaction.

I tell him everything we have learned, and he gets up to pace, his face turning a dull red.

"It seems impossible to believe," he says and then holds up a hand as I frown. "And yet I know Dexar would not send warriors if he did not truly believe the Voildi were a threat. Tell me, why does Dexar care if our tribe falls?"

The question is a fair one. Dexar has historically ignored smaller tribes, trading only with larger tribes who have more to offer— usually located close to his own camp.

"For the Voildi to think that this plan will work, their numbers must be larger than we could have imagined. I believe this plan has been in place for close to one revolution, perhaps even longer, and it is only due to luck that we discovered it now. Your tribe is small; that is true. But if the Voildi took it, they would look to Berax's tribe next. After that, it would likely be Livaq's tribe. And after that, perhaps even Rakiz's tribe."

Tecar ceases his pacing and frowns at me. "It seems unimaginable. The Voildi are a brutal, senseless race with little ability for critical thought. And yet they are suddenly able to organize themselves enough to work together and attack as one?"

I nod. "It's difficult to believe, and yet it remains true. The packs are taking orders from a male named Killis. And according to a Voildi we tortured on the way, Lafa will order his warriors to attack with the Voildi."

The kradi is quiet as each of Tecar's warriors stare at me in stunned silence.

"To turn on his own race for the *Voildi*?" one of Tecar's guards bites out, and I nod.

"You know Lafa has longed for more territory without the warriors to take it. He will split your territory with the Voildi if they do not double-cross him first."

Tecar finally sits, his face hard, shock clear in his eyes. "When do you believe they will attack?"

I shrug, and Tazo shifts, drawing Tecar's attention.

"I believe it will be soon," Tazo says. "By now, they must be aware that we know of their plans. They no longer have the element of surprise, but they know that our defenses are not as strong as we would like. It will take time for warriors from other tribes to travel to this camp. Some will be unwilling to leave their females and children with fewer defenses and may hesitate to join the fight. Others may not truly believe that the Voildi present a threat."

Tecar nods. "Our tribe is small, but our warriors are fierce. We will meet the Voildi with the full force of our rage."

"Dexar is sending warriors to join us, and he has sent messengers to other tribes as well. In the meantime, we must improve your defenses."

At this, Tecar's eyes narrow. "Our camp is well defended."

I do not have the time to spare this warrior's ego, even if

he is a king. I get to my feet. "I studied your camp for barely a few moments, and I could already see more than one opportunity for improvement. On the east side, it's clear to see which kradi is used by the healers, and it is located much too close to the outskirts of the camp. This will be the first kradi to be attacked. It should stay in place, as the Voildi will target it, assuming that they will be able to take out your healers. In the meantime, you will need to remove all sick and injured and shift the healers to a kradi that is more easily defended in the center of the camp."

Tecar grits his teeth and nods. "What else?"

I shrug. "It took too long for your sentries to notice us and react accordingly. They need to be spaced further apart and hidden so they can see the Voildi coming. You must also untie the mishua and allow them to roam free in their pens. If the Voildi get close, the mishua won't hesitate to strike them down. Would you like me to continue?" I raise my eyebrow and attempt to ignore a slight choking sound from Beth as she obviously tries to hold back her laugh.

"No," Tecar grinds out. "This is Yurix, my head of security. He will take your suggestions under advisement." Tecar shifts his gaze to the male who attempted to stop us from entering the camp. The male nods, and then Tecar glances at one of his other warriors, a wide-shouldered male who gives us an easy grin.

"Verkas will show you to a kradi so you can rest, and we will meet in the morning. In the meantime, I must talk with my advisers."

Beth

Verkas is a talker, and he chats to the other warriors while we walk toward the kradis reserved for guests. Zarix is silent apart from the occasional grunt, but he strokes his hand along my lower back as I hobble into the space.

Zarix, Javir, and I will share one kradi, and the other warriors will share another, swapping out so two of them can sleep while the others guard our backs.

Unlike the kradis at Dexar's camp, these are sparsely furnished and decorated. A few chairs sit low to the ground while three sets of furs are lying in different spots along the outer edge of the kradi. Our saddlebags have been placed neatly against one wall, and my knees practically go weak at the idea of clean clothes and a few hours of sleep.

Zarix murmurs in my ear, "Get some rest. I'll be back soon."

Verkas motions to a servant as Zarix leaves me alone. "Inniz will show you where you can bathe if you like?"

"I'd love that." I should be cleaning my stitches more often than I have been, and the last thing I need is to risk a nasty infection.

Javir lays down my crossbow and stares at Inniz suspiciously. He's been quiet since we left, and I haven't wanted to push him.

"I'll come with you," he says, and Inniz simply smiles.

"Of course. The male bathing area is located nearby."

I grab a change of clothes, and we follow Inniz. Luckily, the bathing area is close by, and I feel my eyebrows rise as I take in the hot pools.

"Wow, they look amazing."

Each pool is surrounded by greenery, giving bathers privacy. Inniz leads me to one of the more secluded pools and gestures to where soap and a cloth-like towel have been laid out for me. Then she points to a little bell.

"If you need anything, please ring and someone will come to help you."

"Thank you so much," I say, practically vibrating with the need to get clean.

Tiny wrinkles appear near her large brown eyes as she smiles again, and then she turns, leading Javir away. I listen to them murmuring for a few more moments, and then his low laugh fades into the distance.

I glance around, shrug, and strip. It feels weird to be naked outside, but my need to get clean outweighs my modesty right now.

I sit down on the edge of the pool and pull off the bandage, studying my stitches. The stitches look okay, with none of the angry red that would indicate infection. I avoid poking at it for now and slide my butt over, sinking into the pool.

The water is warm and clean, and I sigh as I slip deeper, dunking my head.

This is the life.

For a moment, I can forget that I'm on a strange planet with a man who makes me question my determination to return to the career that I worked so hard for.

I'm basically at an alien spa, and I'm going to enjoy the hell out of it.

I soap up my hair and rinse it twice. Then I wash every inch of my body. I'm gently cleaning my stitches when female voices sound.

I slap my hands over my breasts and sink deeper in the water as the voices get closer.

A woman laughs, and I hear splashing as someone slips into a pool. Her friend murmurs something, and they must move closer to me because I can hear their conversation.

I almost announce myself, letting them know I'm here, and then I hear it.

"—Zarix," one of them says, her voice young and girlish.

I freeze, slowly moving closer to the voices, careful not to splash and draw attention to myself.

The other woman's voice is throaty. "Mmm, I would love to tumble him."

A snort. "Maybe before all of this. No longer."

"He has no idea, does he?"

"Why would he? Herick disappeared years ago. They probably think he's dead."

"It would be better if he were dead. Imagine the gall of him to join a tribe that would work with the Voildi." Disgust coats her words, and I stare at the water in shock.

They can't possibly be talking about—

"All I want to know is whether these warriors from Dexar's tribe can even be trusted. You know what they say—like father, like son."

The words are in Braxian, but my translator turns them into a saying I've heard many times on Earth. It turns out that people really are assholes everywhere.

This will kill Zarix. The guy is already so hardened by life. He thinks I can't tell that under his rough exterior is a man who has been kicked down by his circumstances and pushes people away because he can't face losing them.

He already carries so much blame for what happened to Hana. What will happen when he finds out that his own father has betrayed his people?

I shift, accidentally banging my leg against the stone side of the pool. I let out a yelp as pain runs up my leg and slap a hand over my mouth as the women's voices go silent.

Shit.

I have a vision of my naked ass flashing through the camp as I attempt to hobble out of here, and I close my eyes. I'm not going anywhere.

After a long, fraught moment, they finally resume their conversation, although their voices are lowered. I blow out a breath and slowly pull myself out of the pool, reaching for the towel.

My mind is racing with my next move. Maybe the women are just gossips, and Zarix's dad has nothing to do with Lafa's tribe.

But what if they're telling the truth and Zarix is about to go to war, with no idea that his father will be on the opposite side? If that's the case, then he'll need a little warning so he can mentally prepare himself.

I pull on my clothes, leaving my leg unbandaged. Elliz gave me some salve to put on the stitches, so I'll do that in the kradi. In the meantime, I have to figure out just exactly what I'm going to tell Zarix.

One thing is for sure—I have to tell him something. Zarix would never tolerate a lie of omission, even if it's with the intention of protecting him.

Zarix is nowhere to be found when I return from my bath. A much sweeter-smelling Javir is curled up, snoring in his furs, and despite myself, I smile.

I must doze off while waiting for Zarix because I jolt when his arms come around me.

"Shh," he whispers. "It's just me."

"I've got something to tell you," I blurt out.

"What?" His voice is low and gruff, and I turn in his arms, blinking up at him.

He looks exhausted.

"Where were you?" I ask instead. "What time is it?"

He shrugs. "Almost dawn."

He's been awake all night, likely finding holes in the camp security.

I snuggle close, closing my eyes. He'll never sleep if I tell him now.

"Never mind," I say. "Let's talk in the morning."

CHAPTER THIRTEEN

Z^{arix}

I GROWL IN SATISFACTION AS I PULL BETH CLOSE, BOTH OF US panting as we recover from our morning tumble. Exploring her delicate body is a million times more invigorating than the scant hours of sleep I have just had. She feels perfect in my arms, and I shake off the thought even as I bury my hand in her long, silky hair.

Beth will leave. Just as everyone else has left me, Beth will return to her planet and to the kind of males who would never think to torture a Voildi for information.

I saw the look in her eyes yesterday. She was revolted—both at the words the Voildi was saying and the actions I took to make him talk.

Usually I would never allow a Voildi to live. But the thought of seeing any more disgust on Beth's face stilled my hand. It was only after, when I imagined the Voildi explaining its injuries to its pack, that I realized death would have been a more merciful end.

Beth is gentle and soft. While she has a smart mouth and a quick wit, she was not made for the harsh realities of this planet and even less so for the reality of life with me.

"Zarix," she begins, and I roll, careful not to knock her leg.

"We need to remove those stitches today," I say, and she nods.

"I'm going to switch to only using one crutch and see how I do. Listen, we need to talk."

I feel a sharp disquiet at her tone, and I lower my head, pressing a kiss to her soft mouth. She relaxes under me, warm and welcoming, and I growl, raising my head as voices sound outside.

The other warriors are waiting, and I must get to work.

"I will be back later," I say, getting to my knees.

She glowers at me and then sighs. "Fine. What will I do today?"

I frown. "I suppose it would be too much to ask you to stay in the kradi where you will be safe?"

"That's right," she says sweetly, but her eyes flash dangerously. A laugh rises in my chest, and the sound seems to echo in the kradi. I cut it off, raising my eyebrows, and Beth snorts even as a slow grin spreads over her face.

"Not used to that, are you?" she teases, and I narrow my eyes back, well aware that the voices have silenced outside. Likely the warriors have died in shock after hearing me show any expression of humor.

"I'm not," I say honestly, reaching for my sword. I slide my feet into my boots, and my whole body aches to rejoin her as she stretches in the furs. Her breasts pop out from beneath the blanket, and my mouth waters for the taste of her small nipples.

"Your cruelty knows no bounds," I say, gritting my teeth as my cock hardens.

"That's what you get for suggesting I stay in this tiny tent all day," she smirks, and I barely resist the urge to kiss the smile off her lush mouth.

"Stay within camp," I say instead, and she nods, the humor leaving her eyes. "I mean it," I say. "One of our warriors should be with you at all times."

She nods again, and I turn, finally making myself leave the kradi to meet Tazo, Perik, and Dekir. All of them examine me as if I have walked out of the kradi without my clothes on.

"What?"

"Nothing," Tazo says after a long moment. "I was simply unaware that you knew how to laugh."

I show him my teeth, and Perik snorts in amusement.

"Let's go" is all I say, striding away.

Beth

I feel like a complete badass as I pick up my crossbow. Shortly after Zarix left, Verkas stopped by our kradi, his eyes twinkling as he checked if I needed anything. I immediately asked for a crossbow lesson, and now we're set up on the other side of the camp, where a large, solid piece of wood hangs from a tree.

Verkas steps forward, adjusting my stance. The majority of my weight is on my right leg, which would leave most people off-balance.

Luckily, as a dancer, I'm used to spending large amounts of time on one leg.

"Okay, now raise the crossbow."

I bring it up, gritting my teeth slightly at the weight of it. I didn't notice how heavy this thing was when I fired it at the Voildi in the tavern, adrenaline taking over.

Right now, muscles in my arms, back, core, and thighs are tense as I work to hold the crossbow steady.

Verkas grins. "You will need to practice holding the weapon for minutes at a time to strengthen these muscles."

I nod. "Okay. Now what?"

"Now, the number one rule when using a crossbow is to always keep your hands under this long piece of wood here. Keep your fingers away from this string."

I stare at the string that creates tension in the crossbow. *Yikes.* After the way I shakily handled this thing at the tavern, I'm lucky I'm not down one finger.

I blow out a breath, and Verkas chuckles.

"Ready?"

I nod, staring past the crossbow and at the target. It's about fifty feet away—much further than the Voildi I shot the last time I fired this thing.

I squeeze the trigger, and we both watch as my bolt sails past the target, hitting another tree.

"Well," Verkas says as I lower the crossbow. "At least you hit *something.*"

I send him a dirty look, and he laughs, gesturing for me to try again.

By the time we're finished, I've hit the board twice, and the trees surrounding it are studded with bolts.

"Wow," a voice says from behind us. "You're really bad at that."

I turn and glower at Javir, who sends me a shit-eating grin. Someone is obviously feeling a little better.

"It's a matter of practice," I sniff. "Give me a few days, and I'll be excellent."

From the look on Javir's face, he doesn't quite believe me, but he begins collecting my bolts and handing them to Verkas, who loads the crossbow and slides the rest of the bolts into the canvas bag.

"Thanks for the lesson." I smile at Verkas, and he winks at me.

"Anytime."

Braxians are flooding into camp as we move back toward our kradi. I keep an eye out for Zarix and spot him talking to Tecar as they watch the warriors arrive. Zarix's dark eyes are hard, but his gaze warms as he turns his head, watching me walk toward him.

"Which tribe are these guys from?" I ask.

"Dexar's. We still have not heard word from the messengers who traveled to Rakiz's tribe. There are three other tribes who have promised to send warriors, but their numbers are low."

I gnaw on my lip. I'm starting to realize just how much danger we could really be in. I'm about to be involved in a battle on an alien planet. But it's Zarix I'm worried about. If I know anything about the warrior, it's that he'll be on the front lines, cutting his way through the Voildi. From the savage expression on his face, he's looking forward to it.

My chest clenches at the thought. What if he gets hurt? What if someone manages to get past his defenses and takes him from me?

Javir moves to Tecar's side, immediately regaling him with a story. I scowl. From the amused look on Tecar's face as he glances at me, I have a feeling Javir is telling him about my lack of skill with the crossbow.

One of Tecar's warriors steps forward to talk to him, and Javir turns away. Perik walks past, and Javir's eyes narrow as he tilts his head, his body tensing as if he's a cat about to pounce on a mouse.

He leaps forward, pulling his knife out of the warrior's pocket. He's not subtle this time though, and Perik turns, his huge hand lashing out to cuff Javir around the head.

Zarix tenses, and then he's there, shoving Javir behind him as he glares at Perik.

"Don't touch the boy," he growls, and Perik's eyes widen in surprise. He glances around, taking in the many eyes on both of them, and then he shrugs, throwing up his hands and walking away.

We're all on edge, none more so than Zarix. I glance up at him as he moves close, gently turning me to face him.

"What's wrong?" he murmurs.

"Nothing."

He gives me a look, but I clamp my mouth shut. The last thing he needs right now is to hear all about how worried I am that he's going to end up seriously hurt or worse.

"What can I do to help?" I ask. With so many warriors flooding in here, surely I can set up some kradis or something.

He opens his mouth, and then we both turn as someone begins shouting.

A warrior is heading toward camp, his mishua galloping past the flood of Braxians. He's pale, and the area goes quiet as he reaches Tecar.

"Voildi," he growls. "An army of them. According to one of our sentries, they're less than three days away."

Tecar nods, sending the warrior into camp to rest and refresh. Then he turns to Zarix.

"It appears you were right," he grits out, and Zarix just nods, his gaze scanning the camp.

We're standing on a small hill and can see most of the camp from here. Dexar's warriors are currently setting up kradis so they have somewhere to sleep, and we watch as the last of the healers leave their kradi, moving to the new one that's more heavily guarded in the center of the camp.

"We need to move the females and children to the safest kradis." Zarix glances at me, and I narrow my eyes at him. If he tries to send me away from him, I'll make him wish he'd reconsidered.

The corner of his mouth tips up as he studies my face. I fold my arms in front of my chest.

"Tell me you won't try to send me away," I say.

He hesitates for a long moment and then finally gives me a sharp nod, although I can see the concession costs him.

"I'll let you get back to work," I say, and he leans down, brushing my mouth with his. My cheeks heat as someone whistles, and I pull away to glower at Javir, who gives us a gap-toothed grin.

"You seem happier," I say as we head back to our kradi.

"My mother managed to get a message to one of Dexar's sentries, who sent it to Zarix. She's okay. She's staying with her friend, and she asked Zarix to keep me safe."

Ah. That explains Javir's constant smirk. Not only is his mom alive, but she's given him permission to hang out with his hero. It must be like Christmas for the brat.

My smile drops as I realize I still haven't told Zarix about his father. I gnaw on my lip again as I slump on my furs, tuning out Javir's gossip.

"What's wrong?" he asks, and I glance across at him.

"Nothing," I sigh. "I just have something to tell Zarix, and it's going to hurt him."

Javir frowns, obviously confused. "Why do you have to tell him, then?"

"Sometimes we have to know the truth, even when the truth hurts."

"Like when I thought my mother was dead?"

I nod. "Even if it hurt, you needed to know what had happened, right?"

He tilts his head. "Is someone from Zarix's family dead?"

I shake my head. "No," I sigh. "But I think Zarix would find that news easier to take."

***

Zarix

After hours of strategizing with Tecar, I find Beth asleep in our furs. I run my gaze over her graceful, long-limbed body and instantly harden. Something about this female makes me lose all reason.

She has been doing nothing except shooting her crossbow, over and over, for hours each day. I haven't missed the fact that Verkas has been the one to teach her. The one to make her smile.

Verkas is the perfect male for a female like Beth. Quick to tease, he always seems on the verge of grinning or laughing at some private joke. He's popular with the females of this camp, flirting good-naturedly with many of them, who blush and giggle in response.

I grind my teeth at the thought.

In contrast, I am known for brooding and for refusing to

take a mate. Females are wary of me. But Beth treats my rare smiles as if I have given her a gift.

If anything happens to her…

She opens her eyes, and I drop to my knees, taking her mouth. She instantly winds her arms around my neck, and I sink into her, wishing we could stay in this kradi and block out the world.

I pull back with a sigh.

"We need to remove the thread," I say, gesturing to her leg. She is already steadier on her feet, putting more weight on her leg each day.

She pouts, and I lean down, nipping at her lower lip.

"You have two choices," I say, my voice rough.

"What's option number one?" Her voice is coy as she pulls me close, running her hands up my back.

"I take you to the healers."

She wrinkles her nose. "And option two?"

"I bring the healers here."

She scowls. "Those options suck. I thought you could do it?"

"I could, but since we're in camp, I'll leave it to those who have more experience."

"I guess I may as well get a little exercise."

I help her to her feet, and she eyes her crutches. "I'm going to see how I do without them," she says. Then she grins up at me, fluttering her eyelashes. "Will you catch me if I fall, cowboy?"

I don't know what a cowboy is, but something about her flirtatious tone and the amusement on her face hits me in the gut. Almost before I know it, I'm grinning back at her.

Her smile drops, but her eyes are lit with laughter as she reaches up and runs her nails under my chin. "You should do that more often."

I lower my head and bury my face in her neck. "You make me want things," I admit, the words almost getting stuck in my throat. "Things I should not want."

She strokes my head, and a low laugh leaves her throat. "I think it's about time you started wanting things," she tells me.

I pull back, memorizing her face. Then I watch her carefully as she limps out of the kradi.

It's not far to the healers' kradi, especially now that it's been moved, but Beth pants quietly, wincing occasionally. I scowl, opening my mouth to suggest I carry her, and she sends me a look.

"Sometimes you have to work through the pain," she says, and I scowl but nod, opening the flap of the kradi.

It's warm and cramped in here, and I make a mental note to check that Tecar has set up other healers' kradis throughout the camp. It's likely that we will have an influx of wounded warriors, and even though my tribe has brought healers and supplies, they are almost guaranteed to be overrun.

One of the healers steps forward, chatting with Beth as she gestures for her to take a seat. I tune out the conversation but crouch, examining the wounds in her leg as the healer removes the bandage.

I'm shaken by the force of the relief that hits me. The wound is not swollen or red, and there are no signs of infection. The healer washes the area, applying something that makes Beth wince but likely sterilizes the wound.

Then she begins cutting the threads and working them out of the skin. She nods when she is finished, obviously pleased, and slathers a thick balm on the wounds before bandaging it again.

"Keep this clean and dry," she says. "Come back if you notice any pain, swelling, or red streaks."

Beth nods. "Thank you."

Despite her protests, I carry her back to the kradi. She reaches for me as I lay her back down in the furs.

"Do you have time for a quickie?"

"A quickie?" I frown in confusion, and Beth winks at me, her quick hands making her meaning clear.

I groan, every muscle in my body tensing. Moving away from the temptation of her body is the most difficult thing I have ever done.

"I promised Tecar I would train with his warriors today," I say. "What will you do?"

She shrugs. "The usual. Get a little exercise, practice with my crossbow."

I nod, pleased that she is working to improve her skill. We don't have much time, but she will at least have that weapon available to her if the camp defenses should fall.

My mood turns dark as I stalk through the camp to the small area that serves as the camp's training arena.

If the camp falls, the Voildi will take pleasure in cutting Beth down. If they don't slaughter her, Lafa's warriors will likely take her for themselves. The thought makes me crazed, and I spend the next few hours sparring with warrior after warrior.

"Pick up your sword!" I roar as one of them falls to the ground. "How will you defend this camp if you can't even defend yourself?"

The warrior grits his teeth and reaches for his sword. He jolts forward, and I step aside, a growl leaving my throat.

"Too slow," I grind out. "Go practice until your enemy can't see your sword coming from yards away."

I spin to fight the next warrior, but there are no more

left. They have either finished their training or have slunk off, unwilling to face me in this mood.

"Are you trying to undermine the morale of this camp?" a deep voice asks, and I whirl, meeting Tazo's gaze.

"Do you have something to say?"

"Yes," he says simply. "Whatever your frustrations, choosing now to vent them on Tecar's warriors is a bad move."

"They're too gods-damned slow," I grind out, and he shrugs.

"Perhaps. But they will live or die by their skills within days. They will not become fast enough to please you within the next few hours. Why don't you tell me why you are fighting with such fury?"

I grind my teeth until my jaw aches. "It's none of your concern."

Tazo shrugs, his shoulders rolling with the movement. "Fine." He steps closer, drawing his sword and throwing it to the ground. "If you're looking to brawl, fight me, then."

I don't even pause to consider and simply drop my sword next to his, nodding.

Tazo is light on his feet for a man of his size, and he hits hard and fast. But he is predictable, and he attacks with the same right hook he favored when we were children.

I block it, landing a fist in his gut. He steps back slightly, but it still forces the air from his lungs.

"You have not changed at all," I say, disgusted.

"Oh," he replies, clamping my arm in a lock and using it to knee me in the balls. "I believe I have a few surprises for you."

I gasp out a curse, and he laughs, lifting his elbow to hit the back of my head as I fold in half. I turn the motion into a roll, coming up behind him and kicking out at the back of his knee.

His leg buckles but holds. However, he's too off balance to counter when I pound an uppercut into his ribs.

"You've gotten faster," he gasps out, twisting around to face me. "You were strong but slow when you left camp."

I scowl at him. "I was never slow."

He grins, obviously pleased that I responded to his taunting. A crowd is gathering, and I grind my teeth as he once again reaches forward with a right hook.

I don't fall for it this time, and he grins, twisting into a backhand, which I barely dodge.

"Why don't we talk about what's really bothering you?" he says, and I lash out, smashing my forehead into his nose.

"Gods' shirts!" he curses as blood drips down his face, and he bares his teeth at me. "Does this work for you? Fighting warrior after warrior, all so you can try to forget that you might actually care about people? And that those people might die?"

I growl, and he laughs, stepping forward with unexpected speed. He manages to throw me, and he's on me before I can roll to my feet. He smashes his fist into my face, and I work one knee up, slamming it into his gut. He growls but hits me again, and I manage to reverse our positions, repaying him with a punch that makes him groan.

"How long?" he demands. "How long will you punish yourself for not saving my sister?"

I roll to my feet, ignoring the gathering crowd. "It was my job to protect her."

He shakes his head, wearily getting to his feet. "That honor was mine, and I failed her too. You think I haven't thought the same? I never blamed you, Zarix. Hana refused to listen. No one could stop her when she made a decision."

I know another female who thinks the same way. Who has the same stubbornness running through her veins.

The thought makes me sick with fear. "You will find three of your best warriors and instruct them to take Beth back to our camp before this battle."

Tazo shakes his head as he wipes blood from his face. "You think this will help? You think you will worry less about your female if she's out of sight?"

"She will be safer away from this camp."

Tazo narrows his eyes at me. "And the boy?"

I grind my teeth. "He will stay. Under guard. The Voildi killed his father and burned his home to the ground. He needs to see us achieve his revenge."

Tazo looks past me, and I turn my head, scowling as I take in the crowd that has formed.

Beth stares at me, crossing her arms. "You said you wouldn't send me away," she says.

"I changed my mind."

"I won't go."

I bare my teeth, infuriated by Tazo, the crowd watching us, and the stubborn female gazing at me with wounded eyes.

"You'll do what I tell you."

Beth looks at me for a long moment. "Don't come to me until you're ready to apologize," she says, turning and walking away.

The crowd collectively inhales, and I raise my head, running my gaze over them. Suddenly many of them have somewhere to be, and I watch as the crowd thins.

Tazo slaps me on the shoulder as he walks past. "You've learned nothing, my friend."

CHAPTER FOURTEEN

B eth

I ATTEMPT TO HOLD BACK MY TEARS, BUT I'M OBVIOUSLY NOT successful, since Javir leaps to his feet when I walk into the kradi, a scowl on his face.

"What's wrong?"

"Nothing. I had a fight with Zarix, that's all."

Javir snorts, immediately disinterested. For some reason, it's his unconcern for anything remotely related to adult relationships that makes me choke out a laugh.

He eyes me like I'm a bomb that's about to go off as I slump down onto my furs.

"I've been gathering information," he announces, and I sigh.

"You know what Zarix said about snooping." I glance away, immediately pissed again. Even saying his name hurts right now.

Javir waves that away. "We could be in trouble," he says, and I sit up straighter.

"What do you mean?"

"No one expected the Voildi to gather in such a huge number. And Rakiz hasn't replied to Dexar's messenger. Some people believe he's waiting until this tribe has been slaughtered and he can take out the Voildi and grow his territory."

I frown. Zarix's voice has always held respect when he talked about Rakiz.

"I'm sure he's coming," I say, and Javir snorts.

"Well, if we don't get more warriors soon, it'll be too late."

My stomach swims at the thought, and I sigh again as I remember the look in Zarix's eyes when he gave me his decree.

I'm trying to give him the benefit of the doubt, since he hasn't allowed himself to care about anyone for so long. I'm well aware that it's his protective instincts that are coming out to play and urging him to send me away.

The problem? He won't talk to me about it. He won't say, "Hey Beth, I'm worried about you. Let's think about a few ways we can make sure you stay safe." Instead, he thinks he can just decide to send me out of camp. I think he knows, deep down, that I wouldn't be any safer away from camp, especially considering how many Voildi are gathering nearby. But his control-freak ways are making him behave like a barbarian.

You dumbass. He is *a barbarian.*

"Beth?"

I blink, and Javir's face comes back into focus.

"You're thinking about Zarix again, aren't you?" He rolls

his eyes and suddenly looks so disgusted that I almost expect him to declare that girls have cooties.

I can't help but grin. "I sure am."

He tilts his head as his wide nose wrinkles, and the dim light highlights the flat, almost poreless nature of his blue skin. "You know, you should just talk to him. Mama always says that communication is the most important part of any relationship." His face turns sad at the mention of his mother, and I lay my hand on his knee.

"She's safe, Javir."

"I know. It's just...that tashiv was all we had. What are we going to do now?"

"I promise it'll be okay. I'll do whatever I can to make sure you guys have somewhere to live. And you know Zarix has your back."

Javir looks at me for a long moment and then gives me a gap-toothed grin, looking strangely angelic and nothing at all like a child who could slit a Voildi's throat.

No matter what happens on this planet, I'm going to make sure this kid and his mom are okay. There has to be some fairness in this universe.

"Voildi!"

We both turn as screams sound, almost tripping over each other as we rush out of the tent. I haul my crossbow into my arms as I move, and then we join the crowd, heading toward the camp entrance.

There are no more warriors joining the camp right now, which is likely why the Voildi has taken his chance. My breath catches in my throat as he gets closer—still far enough away that he'd have a chance of escape.

But only because he's riding a mishua.

The poor thing has only stubs where her horns should

be. The Voildi have tied her mouth closed so she can't bite, but I'm still stunned that they were able to take her.

"She's pregnant," Javir murmurs, and I realize he's right. Her belly is swollen, and the Voildi are using her to send us a message.

We'll take everything you hold dear and break it.

The Voildi stands on the mishua's back—something a Braxian would never do. Zarix and Tecar watch the Voildi with blank faces, and I move closer to them.

"Surrender now," the bastard calls with a grin, showcasing his pointed teeth. "And we will let the females and children live."

I almost roll my eyes. Killis sent this asshole while knowing damn well he wasn't coming back. The Voildi's gaze moves past Tecar, and his eyes narrow, the grin falling from his face as he locks eyes with me.

"You," he hisses, and I frown. The mishua moves forward slightly, and Zarix bares his teeth, moving in front of me.

It hits me. This is Jasit. The Voildi that took me. The one who carried me from the other women. The reason I got stuck in that trap and almost died.

Bile rises as I remember terror. Wondering if we'd be eaten. Not wanting to split up from the other women, jumping into that river and knowing I might die. That last, panicked run through the forest.

"You killed my friend," Jasit hisses, and for a moment, the rest of the world falls away and it's just him and me.

I glance down at the mishua, who is practically vibrating, her red eyes glowing with what seems to be rage.

I nip in front of Zarix, ignoring his low growl. Then I raise my crossbow and let my bolt fly.

It goes through Jasit's throat, and he falls from the mishua, choking on his own blood.

"That's called karma, bitch."

The mishua immediately stomps him until he stops twitching, and warriors rush forward to take her into camp. She allows it, although none of them are stupid enough to remove the rope from around her mouth just yet.

Tecar turns and stares at me, raising his eyebrow. Maybe I wasn't supposed to do that.

My bad.

"Sorry," I say, conscious of Javir cracking up beside me. A male I haven't yet met lets out a low growl.

"We could have used him."

Zarix pulls me close while Tecar sighs.

"Killis wouldn't have sent him if he had any useful information." Tecar glances at me. "A female killing a Voildi? At least it's good for camp morale." He narrows his eyes. "But next time, ask first."

I nod, wiggling out from under Zarix's arm. He stares down at me, and I raise my eyebrows.

"I have yet to hear an apology," I say, and Tecar laughs softly, moving off to do whatever tribe kings do in times of war.

Zarix looks at me, and for a second, his eyes are full of torment.

"What's wrong?" I ask.

He glances around, and I notice other warriors giving him the side-eye. He moves through the crowd, gently pulling me after him.

We head back to the kradi and sit on the furs.

Zarix is silent for a long moment, and I reach for his hand.

"My father may be a traitor," he finally says, his expression lost. My eyes fill with tears as I take in his pain.

"How did you find out?"

"Tecar told me he may have been sighted riding with Lafa's warriors." He tilts his head as he studies my face, pulling his hand from mine. "You don't seem surprised by this."

I sigh. "I heard two women talking in the bathing pools the other day. I was going to talk to you, but you came to bed late, and then we both just got busy."

His face is blank, and I frown at him as he gets to his feet. "I need to get back to work," he says.

"Zarix—"

He turns and walks away, and I narrow my eyes at his retreating back. Should I have told him earlier? For sure. But if Zarix wants someone to blame for this shitshow, he can blame his father. I grind my teeth as he disappears between two kradis. I'm being pretty damn patient with him, and I'm giving him a break, since I know he's struggling with the idea that his father could betray his people. But if he thinks he can pull away from me, he's about to learn differently.

I blow out a breath. I'll give him some space. For now.

I mope. There's no other word for it. I spend an hour attempting to hit the target with my bolts, grinding my teeth when some of them miss the board completely. My concentration is shot, and I'm cursing as I collect my bolts when Tazo appears.

"You can aim better than that."

"Yeah, no shit." I glower at him over my shoulder, and he grins, unconcerned.

"That shot earlier was a thing of beauty," he marvels, and I nod.

"Thanks."

"So how come you're shooting worse than the first time you picked up a crossbow?"

"The first time I picked up a crossbow, I shot a Voildi at point-blank range."

Tazo grins. "Ah, Zarix told me about that. Obviously you're someone who shoots best under pressure."

I tilt my head as I give up on my practice, shoving bolts into the thin bag.

Tazo moves closer, frowning as my shoulders slump. "You want to talk about it?"

I shrug. "It's not important."

"It obviously is if you're this upset. Go on, I'm good at listening." He grins again and curses as his lip splits.

"Who beat you up?"

"Who do you think?"

I sigh, and Tazo laughs.

"Let me guess, your warrior is the reason for your bad aim."

I glower at him. "Keep annoying me and you'll see how bad my aim really is."

He laughs again but takes the bag from me, helping me collect the last of the bolts.

I frown. "It's just...one thing after another for us. For a couple of days, it seemed like we could actually *be* something, but now all we do is fight."

Tazo nods. "Few things test a relationship—any relationship—more than war, sickness, or famine."

"I know, and I know that what's happening right now isn't exactly normal. But shouldn't we be sticking together during the hard times? Instead, I'm either pissed at him, or he's pissed at me, or both."

Tazo gestures at an overturned log, and I move toward it.

My limp is less pronounced today, and I'm finally moving around without stabbing pain.

I'm still grateful to sit down though, and I reach for a gorgeous purple wildflower, jolting as Tazo slaps my hand away.

"Poisonous to the touch," he says, and I almost laugh. Of course it is.

Tazo smirks, and then his expression turns serious. "Zarix was my best friend when we were young warriors," he says, and I nod. "We were closer than friends, more like brothers. Zarix never knew true family after his mother died and his father left the tribe. He was given to his mother's sister, Mari, who had raised her children and wanted no more. My parents treated him like one of their own when he was near. But Zarix...something inside him never truly believed that he was deserving of love or loyalty. When we were caught breaking the rules, he would immediately claim it was all his idea, taking the blame along with whatever punishment he was given."

Tazo leans over and picks a delicate white flower, offering it to me. I hesitate, and he grins.

"You're learning." He presses it into my hand and then continues with his story. "It quickly became a game to some of the other young boys. To find out just how much Zarix would take. He was always a large, capable fighter, and some were jealous of his abilities with a sword. So they would find a way to break a camp rule and blame Zarix, who would never say anything."

I frown, unable to reconcile this *victim* with the man who refuses to play with others.

Tazo nods, reading my mind. "It never mattered, you see. The punishments. Zarix wanted to be the best warrior in camp. And for a warrior, honor is everything. Those that tormented him, they may have been children, but members of our tribe have long memories, and they are still not well-liked to this day."

I scowl. "Good."

Tazo nods and continues. "One day, Dexar, Zarix, and I broke a rule. A rule that could have gotten all of us killed. Zarix was just another child, but my father was best friends with the tribe king, and Dexar was the tribe king's son and future ruler. Mari immediately blamed Zarix, who didn't say a word to contradict her. She was used to him being in trouble, you see. Dexar and I protested, but it seemed as if once again, Zarix would be held responsible. And then my sister appeared."

Tazo's brow lowers, and I reach for his hand.

"It still hurts," he murmurs.

I nod. "Sometimes I'll think, 'I need to tell my mom that,' or, 'My dad will know how to do this.' I don't know if it'll ever get better."

Tazo sighs. "It helps. Having people who understand. Hana was usually with us when we were kids. She was constantly following us around. That day, I'd sent her off crying because we were planning to try to ride a mishua."

I burst out laughing at the thought. "How old were you guys?"

"Seven summers." Tazo grins at my laugh. "Yes, we all thought we were fierce warriors, held back from our greatness by aging males who refused to allow us to reach our full potential."

My mouth drops open, and Tazo nods.

"Yes, that's how my mother looked when Dexar proclaimed exactly that to his father. Anyway, Hana knew who had decided to ride the mishua—and it wasn't Zarix. He came along, but it was Dexar who wanted to be the youngest warrior ever to sit on a mishua. Hana told the tribe king this. And then she told him what had been happening—that Zarix had been taking the blame for everything that went wrong in the camp."

"What did the tribe king do?"

"Sentenced us to a month cleaning up after the mishua."

"All of you?"

He nods. "Dexar knew not to expect special treatment because he was the tribe king's son, and he would have found a lesser punishment insulting. Zarix was given the punishment because he had not been honest. The tribe king told him that honor doesn't mean allowing your friends to use you."

"What did Zarix say?"

"He said no one used him. It was his choice to cover for those under his protection."

My mouth drops open again. "He said that?"

Tazo smiles. "Dexar and I were disgusted at the decree. We didn't need to be protected, of course. But in Zarix's mind, it was his duty to keep others safe." The smile drops from Tazo's face. "He always thought he was disposable. Always thought we could do without him."

I'm slowly starting to understand the man Zarix has become. "And then Hana died."

Tazo nods. "And then she died. Zarix would have blamed himself no matter what, but in his mind, it was his harsh words that caused her actions that day. This planet rests on Zarix's shoulders, you see."

Tazo's voice is sarcastic, and I sigh, staring down at the white flower in my hand.

At a young age, Zarix lost his parents and was given to a woman who had no use for him. He decided his only role was to protect those he deemed more important than himself. And then Hana died, and he realized he had failed at the only thing he was any good at. So he left. He tried to stop caring, although the fact that he's here, trying to protect this tribe while simultaneously attempting to send me away, shows that he's still that same protector through and through.

He never wanted the responsibility that comes from caring about anyone else. That's why he was so resentful of Javir and me even as we wormed our way under his defenses. He must feel exactly like that orphaned kid. *Disposable.* Now he's learned that his scumbag father has betrayed his tribe and is about to wage war on Tecar.

My face heats with rage, and Tazo smiles sadly at me, letting go of my hand as I get to my feet.

"Thank you for telling me this," I say, and he nods as I turn to walk away.

It's time for Zarix to learn that he's not disposable at all.

CHAPTER FIFTEEN

Z arix

I WAIT UNTIL BETH IS ASLEEP BEFORE I MOVE INTO THE KRADI. I could sleep elsewhere, but even now, I need to be close to her.

I didn't think my gut could twist and my chest could ache the way it does now. Already Tecar's warriors are glancing at me with mistrust in their eyes. They wonder if I am working with my father and if I am setting them up to fail. All the changes I have made to increase the security of this camp are worth nothing now.

I am worth nothing now.

Beth did not want to tell me of what she had heard, and I can understand her hesitation. But the lack of honesty between us chafes.

The remaining warriors from our camp have arrived. Dexar has sent more than I had imagined and has likely needed to order some of his hunters back to help protect our camp.

Unfortunately, the numbers are not enough. Rakiz has not sent word about whether he will be sending some of his warriors, and the Voildi are now close enough that they will likely attack tomorrow. They have gathered on the east side of Tecar's camp—something Tecar expected given the strategic location of his camp. To the west, a mountain range would slow any incoming forces. To the north, a wide river runs, which would leave the Voildi open and vulnerable if they attempted to cross it.

And to the south, Rakiz's camp lies. Although it is several days away, his sentries would have noticed any Voildi marching toward this camp. Hopefully, his honor would prevent him from ignoring the threat. However, Rakiz has still not sent a messenger.

I realize what I'm doing, focusing on strategy so I don't need to think about my father, who left me behind even as I grieved for my mother, his mate. I don't understand how he could have chosen this path. In our camp, he had people who knew my mother, people who grieved with him. I can understand a grieving warrior who hunts alone—as I have for all these years. But I would never leave my child behind without a word. And I can't imagine joining a tribe like Lafa's.

Beth stirs, and I freeze as she opens her eyes.

"You're thinking too loudly," she says. Then realization crosses her face, and she firms her jaw, sitting up as she stares at me.

"I'm sorry I woke you."

She narrows her eyes. "You're pulling away from me. Why?"

"We don't have time for this conversation," I say. "We both need to get some rest."

"Don't be a coward," she snaps, and I slam my jaw closed, clenching my teeth. She gives me a knowing look, tilting her head. "Look," she says. "I'm sorry about your dad. But you have to know that his actions have nothing to do with you."

I can't hold back the growl that's ripped from my throat. "Already males I will fight next to, males I may *die* with, believe I'm just like my father. They wonder if I am working with him."

Beth moves closer, and I close my eyes at the sympathy on her face.

"Then they're fucking idiots," she says, her voice harsh. I open my eyes, and her expression is no longer sympathetic. It's furious. "And don't talk about dying, asshole."

I throw up my hands, but I keep my voice low as I note Javir's soft snores on the other side of the kradi. "You should be with someone who still has honor," I grind out. "Someone like Verkas."

Her mouth drops open, shock and hurt replacing her fury. "You don't want me anymore?"

I push down the instant denial. "This isn't about what *I* want. It's about what is best. Verkas is well liked. He makes you smile." I bite out the words and attempt to ignore the pain in Beth's eyes. "He is respected and honorable."

"I'm trying to be understanding right now, but you're being a giant dick."

I say nothing, and Beth gets to her knees. Her face is pale, eyes lit with fury.

"I don't *need* a man," she spits. "I *chose* you, although this bullshit is making me question that decision. If I wanted to be with someone else, I would. So don't fucking tempt me to find someone who makes me feel like more than an inconvenience or a spare part."

"You lost your world. Your...dancing. You were looking for something to make you feel, and you found me. But that was a mistake."

Beth gives me a long look, and I almost glance away from the disappointment in her eyes.

"If that's what you really think, then you're right. I did make a mistake."

She turns away, lying back down in the furs, and I do the same, staring at the dull brown walls of the kradi for the rest of the night.

***

Beth

My throat is hoarse, eyes red from crying, and I barely have the willpower to get out of bed. Zarix was gone when I woke, so I must have drifted off at some point after we both lay awake in silence for hours after our discussion.

Earlier, Javir scurried into our kradi, face pale and eyes wild as he told me just how many Voildi have now gathered in full view of the camp.

Thousands.

There are thousands of Braxians too, but many of them are women and children, and from the frightened look on Javir's face, we're hopelessly outnumbered.

I finally summon the will to get up and wish I could climb back into bed. The Braxians are quiet and somber, and I trudge to the camp entrance, where I stare at the thousands of Voildi, all lined up in the distance. Between them, I can see larger warriors, likely the Braxians from Lafa's tribe.

"Why haven't they attacked yet?"

I didn't realize I spoke aloud, but Perik steps up behind me. The look on his face is strange, his expression one I can't quite place, and I frown at him.

"They're waiting," he says, his eyes on the Voildi in the distance.

"Waiting for what?"

He glances at me as if surprised I'm still talking. His face clears as he shrugs. "Probably for more Voildi."

"There are more of them?"

"There are more Voildi than Braxians could ever have imagined. The tribes never knew this because Voildi have never worked together before."

I shudder, turning to walk through the camp. I have a vague idea of practicing with my crossbow some more, but I freeze as joyous shouts sound from the south side of the camp.

I can't see over the huge Braxians, so I move into one of the gathering spots and climb onto a boulder.

What. The. Hell.

Hundreds of Braxian warriors are pouring into the camp.

"Rakiz," someone says, relief coating the word. "It's Rakiz's tribe."

Tecar appears, stepping forward to greet a couple of warriors on a mishua.

One of them slides down, and my mouth drops open. It's one of the human women from the ship. The one who was looking after Charlie...Nevada, I think. She's dressed in leather pants and carrying a sword, and she grins as the huge warrior dismounts, wrapping his arm around her shoulders as he speaks to Tecar.

I elbow my way through the crowd, and her eyes go wide as she sees me.

"Holy crap," she says, and both men turn as she dances forward. "Beth, right?"

I'm laughing, nodding my head, almost crying as we hug. She glances around at the gathering crowd, and I tense as I meet Zarix's gaze. His expression is tormented as he looks at me, and then Tecar says something, drawing his attention, and he glances away.

"Do you have somewhere private we can talk?" Nevada asks.

"I sure do." I lead her to our kradi. "We share this with Javir, a kid we collected on our travels," I say. "He's usually out roaming the camp, so we should have the space to ourselves."

We step inside, and Nevada makes herself at home, sitting cross-legged on the furs. "So," she says, "tell me everything."

"Well, you obviously know that we were taken in the fight. We made a deal that if one of us had a chance to escape, we'd do it." My eyes fill with tears. "I left them behind."

Nevada reaches out, pulling me down to sit next to her. "I have good news.

"Oh yeah?"

"Ivy managed to get free."

"Oh my God. That's great."

Nevada grins. "You know the leader of the Voildi? The one who managed to get them all to work together?"

I nod.

"Well, Ivy took his eye. Idiot's left looking like a yellow

Patchy the Pirate. Oh, and Zoey? We rescued her. She had pneumonia from the damage to her ribs and the bad condition she was kept in, but she's slowly getting better, and the healers think she'll be okay."

I'm weak with relief. Okay, we have no idea where Ivy is, but Nevada's right—she's tough. Especially if she managed to get free *and* hurt Killis in the process.

Nevada stretches out her long legs, crossing them at the ankles. "So now we just need to find out if Charlie's still alive, kidnap Alexis out of Dexar's camp, and get you guys back to the spaceship so you can skedaddle out of here."

"Um. You don't plan on leaving?"

Nevada waves her hand. "Nah. I'm happy with my honey-bunny. We're even mated and everything." She holds up her wrist, and I stare at the gorgeous gold band encircling it. I've seen those bands before but never thought to ask Zarix what they mean.

"Mated?"

"Yeah, you know, it basically means we're married."

"So you're like a queen now?"

"Yup. And I didn't even have to marry a balding playboy to make it happen."

She winks at me, and I can't help but laugh. My head is whirling with the influx of information.

"What about the other women?" I ask.

"Oh." She snaps her fingers. "Ellie's pregnant. So she's not going to be joining your girls' trip either. That's why she's not here, by the way. She needs to stay close to camp and the healers. Vivian wants to go home, and I know Alexis was working for NASA or some shit, so she's probably not a fan of the whole backward, barbarian planet thing. And if Charlie's still alive, I bet she'll be the first one on that ship."

She frowns, her face falling, and we sit in glum silence

for a moment. Then she raises one eyebrow as a thought obviously occurs to her.

"How did you end up here anyway?"

I blurt it all out. How Zarix found me in the trap, took me to the healers, and then took me back to his camp. Nevada's gaze narrows, and I frown at her.

"What?"

"You were in Dexar's camp? You saw Alexis?"

"I did."

"Was she okay?"

"Yeah, for sure. Dexar seems to be treating her okay, and I think she was bored more than anything."

"Okay. If we live through this battle, I'mma need you to give me the lowdown on that security. Ellie and I may not be going with you guys, but we're gonna help you all get back to Earth."

Both of us turn as Javir walks in, meeting my gaze.

"You think you can return to your planet?" he asks.

Nevada gives him a look that would intimidate me. "Snitches get stitches," she says.

Javir merely sneers at her, showcasing the gaps where his front fangs should be, and she laughs.

"You must be Javir."

Javir bares more of his teeth, eyes narrowed. "Who wants to know?"

Nevada lets out a laugh. "I like this kid."

I get to my feet, sending him a warning look. "This is Rakiz's mate," I tell him. "The tribe queen."

He pales slightly but glowers at her some more and then turns, silently walking out the door.

"I don't know what's gotten into that kid," I murmur, and Nevada laughs.

"Come on. Let's go kick some Voildi ass."

Beth

I was prepared for the fear. The knee-weakening terror. The bargaining with gods I've never believed in.

You know what I wasn't prepared for?

The boredom.

It's been two days since Nevada arrived, and while there have been a few skirmishes as the Voildi test our defenses, nothing big has happened yet. Apparently Rakiz has sent messengers to other tribes, but they're located far enough away that this downtime is actually a good thing when it comes to building our army.

The problem?

If we don't engage with the Voildi sometime soon, we could end up running out of supplies. There are a lot of mouths to feed, and we can't risk sending out too many hunters.

It's a tense kind of boredom. While the arrival of Rakiz and his warriors has lightened the mood slightly, we're all well aware of the stakes. People will die in this battle, and the thought makes my palms sweat and my mouth dry.

Zarix has climbed into our furs each night, pulling me close. We don't talk—both of us unwilling to spend the few precious moments we have together fighting. He hasn't tried to send me away again. By now, he knows I'm safer here, although I often catch him staring at me, his expression agonized as our gazes meet.

I want to shake him, to make him admit that he's afraid of caring, of being vulnerable, and that it's affecting what little time we could have left together.

But I fell for a stubborn warrior. I've realized that now.

He did what the few silk-tongued men I dated on Earth could never have done—he showed me that there is still life to be lived after ballet, even when I didn't particularly want to live it.

"Beth?"

I turn and meet Nevada's inquiring look. She hands me a piece of wood, and I pass it along to one of the warriors. Apparently this camp is in a strategic location, but Tecar hasn't been taking advantage of it properly. He has no real lookout, so while the camp entrance is on a small hill, Nevada has us building some guard towers which will help us defend the camp when the time comes.

Nevada looks past me, where Zarix has turned away. She lifts one eyebrow. "You want to talk about that good-looking son of a bitch?"

"It's complicated."

She laughs. "Been there. It was complicated for Rakiz and me as well."

"How did you fix it?"

"He tried to step down as tribe king for me."

I sigh, depressed. "Zarix tried to send me away to 'protect me.' Then he suggested I move on with another man because he is well liked, respectful, and honorable."

Nevada winces. "Ouch."

"Yeah. He just found out some news about his father that upset him, and instead of talking about it, he's pushing me away. I don't know how to get through to him."

"Here's the thing. These warriors aren't like human men. They seriously believe that it's their job to keep us safe. It sounds like Zarix is similar to Rakiz in a lot of ways—both believe they're responsible for our safety. We have to slowly get them to see things our way."

She grins at me, stepping back. I mull over her words as

we watch the warriors load a bunch of small, round objects into large crates.

Nevada raises her voice. "I need torches burning at each of these points, but for the love of God, don't let them get near these pods until I say so."

She gazes around with a steely-eyed stare, and the warriors nod.

"What do the pods do?" I ask, leaning closer. They look like bunches of small coconuts, but the warriors are handling them as gently as if they're newborn babies.

Nevada smirks. "Trelga tree pods," she says. "You'll see." She turns her head, pointing at the hastily constructed wall that has been built around the camp. "This needs to be fortified," she says, and one of the warriors nods, respect in his eyes.

"How'd you get them to listen to you?" I ask quietly, and she raises her eyebrow.

"I've been completely focused on camp security almost since I arrived. There was resistance at first, but these guys know all the changes were for the best, right, Hewex?"

He nods, grins, and gets to work fortifying the wall.

"Impressive," I murmur, and she smiles.

"Wow," she says, the smile dropping from her face. "Who's that?"

I turn, raising my eyebrows. Around us, the camp goes quiet as the huge warrior rides through the south entrance. Everything about him is just *big*. His mishua stands a head above most of the others I've seen, her massive body prowling forward, lethal horns catching the light. I wouldn't be surprised if she breathes fire.

The warrior himself is also somewhat oversized. I've gotten used to being a midget on this planet, but this guy is bigger than most of the other warriors here. A long scar winds down the side of his face close to his ear, traveling down toward his neck. Despite the scar, his face is handsome and oddly compelling.

He nods at Rakiz and dismounts, boots hitting the ground with a thud.

Hewex leans close. "His name is Vrex. He belongs to no tribe, although technically he was born under Dexar's father's rule. Now he lives alone, choosing to hunt when necessary and occasionally stepping in when needed for battles such as this one."

"So he's a mercenary?" Nevada asks.

Hewex shrugs. "His loyalty is to those he judges as worthy, and he lives by his own code."

Nevada glances at me. "Are you thinking what I'm thinking?"

"I don't think anyone is ever thinking what you're thinking."

She grins, and my mouth drops open as she stalks over to where Rakiz is deep in conversation with Vrex. Zarix stands next to Rakiz, listening, and his gaze meets mine as I jolt into action and follow Nevada.

"Who sent a messenger to you?" Rakiz's voice is curious, and Vrex shrugs.

"I chose to come."

Rakiz nods, and that seems to be the end of their discussion as Nevada sidles closer.

"Sup," she says. "Thanks for coming." She glances at Rakiz, who pulls her close. "Can I interrupt for a moment?"

"Of course," Rakiz says, his tone indulgent. He looks at Nevada as if she's the reason for the stars in the sky, and my heart twists.

I can feel Zarix's gaze on me, but I avoid looking at him

for now. It hurts too much to know that we could have this. If only we could both get our shit together.

Nevada turns back to Vrex, and I let my gaze run over his body. Everything about him screams that he's someone you don't want to fuck with. He's dressed in unrelenting black and built like he's been popping steroids his whole life. He glances at me, and I almost shiver as I meet his gaze. His eyes are such a light amber that they appear almost gold as he glances away disinterestedly.

A warm arm wraps around my waist, and I breathe in Zarix's scent. For whatever reason, he's feeling territorial, and I sigh.

"I'd like to hire you," Nevada tells Vrex, and Rakiz raises one eyebrow. Good to know that even he has no idea what's going through his mate's head at any given time.

Vrex raises his arm, running it down his mishua's neck, and she preens at the attention.

"What task is it that you need?" he finally asks.

"Karja," Rakiz says warningly, and Nevada turns in his arms, raising one hand to his face. They seem to block out the world as they stare into each other's eyes.

"I need to do this," she says softly. "Please."

One sharp nod from Rakiz, and it's decided. The mercenary doesn't miss any of this, his eyes narrowing slightly as he takes in the couple.

Nevada glances at me, her expression suddenly uncertain, and I nod. I see where she's going with this, and it makes sense. I have a feeling that this scary, deadly warrior is our best shot at finding the other women.

"We are from another planet," I say, and Nevada shoots me a grateful look. "We were separated from each other, and I was kidnapped by the Voildi along with two other women.

One of them is safe now, but the other one is responsible for the damage to Killis's eye."

Vrex's head tilts slightly at this, and for the first time, I see a hint of interest on his face.

Nevada clears her throat. "Her name is Ivy. She was last seen when she escaped from the Voildi. Will you help us find her?"

Vrex is silent for a long moment, and Zarix leans close, murmuring into my ear.

"Breathe," he says, and I blow out the breath I was holding.

Vrex glances at me again and then turns his attention back to Rakiz. "If I do this, you will owe me one favor, due at the time of my choosing."

Rakiz clenches his jaw but finally nods, and Vrex bows his head.

"It is done."

I meet Nevada's eyes, and she's back to looking uncertain. It's suddenly clear why Vrex is considered such a threat. How many other tribe kings owe him favors on a planet where honor is everything? And what will this warrior use those favors for when he's ready to call them in?

Zarix steers me away from the group, and I look up at his tight jaw.

"What's wrong?"

"Our spies have determined that the Voildi will attack tomorrow morning, likely in the early hours. We have let them assume that our camp is slow to rouse and have been careful to keep our warriors out of sight during this time."

I shiver, as I realize what this means. This time tomorrow, we could all be dead. No more wisecracks from Nevada. No more pickpocketing from Javir. No more kisses or heated looks from Zarix.

He turns to me, reading my mind. "Will you spend this night with me?"

I know what he's asking. Will I push all our relationship problems to the side, choose not to pick a fight, and spend the next few hours with him before he goes into battle?

"Of course."

CHAPTER SIXTEEN

B^{eth}

It's still dark when Zarix gently lifts me off him. Last night, Nevada arranged for Javir to be watched so that we could have some privacy. We ate dinner together, talking about everything except the upcoming battle. I told him about ballet, even going as far as to show him a few positions, slowly twirling before I raised my injured leg above my head.

My muscles stretched, feeling tight after weeks without dancing but still responding instantly. I was taking it very easy, careful not to overwork my healing leg.

Zarix's eyes darkened as he watched me twist and turn. His jaw tightened as I moved onto tiptoe, on my right leg, slowly raising my arms as I danced to music that I could only hear in my head.

Then I was laughing in surprise as he snatched me out of the air, rolling me beneath him and murmuring words too low for my translator to pick up as he kissed his way down my body.

We made love for hours. The last time, he stared deep into my eyes as I choked back a sob, barely restraining the urge to beg him not to fight in the morning. He's a warrior, a barbarian who was built for this, but it doesn't make it any easier.

"I love you," I whispered as he thrust, my breath catching as he ground into me, so deep it was as if he was trying to imprint his body into mine.

He slammed his mouth into mine, his huge body trembling as we found completion together.

Now he's going to war.

I reach for my own clothes, and we dress silently. Zarix's mind is already on the battle ahead, but he pulls me close as we get to our feet. He hands me my crossbow and nods approvingly as I slide the piece of armor beneath my dress.

According to Nevada, the stunning blue-green material is actually a dragon scale, which is why it's large enough to cover my entire chest and stomach. It molds itself to my body, and I blow out a breath. We all have our part to play in this battle, and Nevada told me I wouldn't be playing any part at all unless I wore this scale.

I follow Zarix out of the kradi, reaching for Javir as he walks toward us. I wrap my arms around him and squeeze. He lets out a sound like a pissed-off cat but allows it, his arms finally coming around my waist.

"You'll stay with the healers, right?"

He nods, and I pull back, staring down at him. "Promise?"

He nods again, and I sigh. By now, I'm well aware that Javir has problems with impulse control. While he may be promising to stay safe now, and he may mean it with every inch of his body, the fact remains that he can't be trusted to keep himself safe.

I glance at Zarix, who nods. Perik has promised to watch Javir for the entirety of the battle. He's one of the warriors in charge of guarding the healers' kradi, and after traveling with us, he'll know that he needs to keep Javir within sight.

"Be careful," Javir says solemnly. I nod and give him a grin, patting the scale beneath my dress. "Nevada's got me covered. I'll see you later, okay?"

He turns to Zarix, and the males stare at each other for a long moment.

"I'll make them pay for what they did to your father," Zarix says. "But you're of no use to anyone if you're dead."

Javir nods. "Fight well," he says as Zarix slaps him on the shoulder, and then he's off and running toward the healers' kradi.

Zarix turns me and takes my mouth in a deep kiss, and then we move away to our respective posts, so many words unsaid and yet nothing left to say.

Nevada is stalking along the east walls, hissing orders as everyone falls into place. Everyone in this camp has been forbidden from using any fire this morning, and voices are allowed to be no louder than a murmur as we lull the Voildi into believing that most of the camp is still sleeping.

We line up at our posts, and the faces around me are grim as we stay hidden behind the wall. Most of these Braxians are older, although some were chosen for their ability to aim over a long distance. There are even a few other women, although most of them will be tasked with handing out supplies as they get low.

I peer through a crack in the stone, and we wait silently for what seems like hours.

The waiting is the worst part. I'm almost anxious for the

Voildi to attack, if only to replace some of the terror with adrenaline.

It's as if the thought conjures the Voildi, and I narrow my eyes as I see movement in the dim light. Nevada moves up beside me, and we both peer into the distance as the Voildi get closer.

The plan relies on patience, and it's evident from the shuffling feet behind me that most Braxians aren't real familiar with the word. Nevada turns her head, and the shuffling immediately ends.

"Closer," she murmurs as we watch. "A little closer."

It feels like they're almost on top of us, but we need to lure them in for our plan to have the best chance of working. Still, we barely move, watching as the dark night lightens to a dull gray, and the Voildi come into view, lined up and marching, swords in their hands.

I tremble, and Nevada grins at me, her eyes wild.

"Bet you never imagined this when we were huddled in the cage on that ship," she murmurs, and then she steps back, her gaze running over the warriors.

"Get in place," she hisses, and the Braxians move as one, eyes lit from within as they finally get to see battle.

They crouch on the large posts, no more than five feet between them. Muscles tremble as they restrain themselves, waiting for Nevada's signal.

The Voildi are now so close that I can see individual faces, and I stare at Nevada, willing her to make the call.

She's a marine, which means she knows what she's doing. But my heart is racing, blood pounding a beat in my ears as we watch them come even closer.

"Light it up, bitches!" Nevada roars, and the warriors grab the torches, holding them to the Trelga pods, which they haul at the incoming army.

Holy shit. They're explosives.

Body parts fly, and their front line fractures as they realize what's happening. The Voildi split, attempting to dodge the Trelga pods, but the Braxian warriors throw like pro baseball players, the packed muscles of their arms allowing them to let the pods fly with a force I couldn't have imagined.

Nevada glances across at me, a grim smile on her face. "Your turn. Hit 'em hard, Beth."

I step up beside her, lifting my crossbow. At every internal post, next to the pod-throwers, warriors reach for longbows and crossbows, waiting silently, poised and ready.

I attempt to block out the Voildi's screams as they die, burning.

They'd kill you and eat you, Beth. Get your fucking head in the game.

One of them charges past the front lines, making his way toward the camp.

"Hold," Nevada orders, and I grit my teeth as he gets closer and closer. Smoke is thick in the air, the smell of burning flesh mingling with the heady, strangely fresh scent of the pods.

"Hold," Nevada repeats, and then more Voildi charge past their front line with a roar.

"Fire!" Nevada screams, and I block out everything but the Voildi closest to us, picturing my bolt going straight through his left eye.

I miss.

He weaves to the side, and then his teeth are bared as he lifts his sword, charging closer until he can't be more than fifty feet away.

My next bolt hits his chest. He screams and goes down, but I'm already aiming and firing at the next, and the next.

It becomes almost routine, and I systematically shoot and kill as one of the Braxian women passes me bolts until there are no more bolts left. Nevada nods at me, and I climb down, feeling stunned and out of it, almost as if I'm sleep-walking.

Now it's time for the mounted Braxians to play their part.

My heart slams a heavy beat in my chest, and my stomach clenches as I scan the crowd of warriors waiting near the camp entrance. Zarix meets my gaze, his mishua shifting her feet impatiently as they prepare for Tecar's signal. On the other side of camp, Rakiz is readying his warriors to charge and circle behind the Voildi so we can attack them from both sides.

Fuck it.

I sprint toward Zarix, ignoring Nevada's hand reaching for my arm. His eyes widen, and then he reaches out, lifting me onto his mishua. He buries his hand in my hair, pulling me close, his arms so tight that he's almost crushing me in his embrace.

"Stay safe," I murmur as he pulls away. "I mean it, Zarix."

"I'll be fine," he says. Suddenly there are no hurt feelings between us, and nothing else matters except the fact that this could be the last time we speak.

That reminds me.

I reach beneath my dress, and Zarix's eyes widen as I pull out the dragon scale.

"Take this."

"No."

"Zarix."

"You wear it."

I grind my teeth. "I'm going to be safe, hiding with everyone else in camp. You take it. Please. For me."

Zarix reaches out, wiping tears off my face. He stares at me for a long moment. "You need this from me?"

I nod. "I know it's small on you, but just wear it over your heart or something. A little protection is better than none at all."

He takes the scale, but I can see that the effort costs him, a muscle ticking away in his left cheek.

"You will stay with Nevada," he orders, and I nod. He looks over my head at Nevada, who must also nod because he finally sighs, shoving the scale beneath his shirt, where it covers his heart.

"I'm sorry for not being the male I should have been for you," he murmurs, staring into my eyes. And for a moment, there's no battle, no Voildi, no camp, just us.

"You're exactly the male I need."

He smiles at me, and it's sad. "I love you."

My cheeks are wet with tears, and I let out a hoarse laugh as I wipe them away. "Your timing is impeccable," I say. "I love you too. Now don't get dead."

He doesn't bother promising to stay alive. We both know it's a promise he might break. Instead, he stares at me for one long moment, his gaze darting over my face. He brushes my hair back behind my ear and then helps me swing down from the mishua. I move back toward Nevada as Tecar glances at the warriors waiting for his signal. He raises his arm, and everyone goes silent.

"Today we show the Voildi that we do not fear them. We show traitors to our people that their betrayal will not be rewarded. Today we will make sure that any Voildi who happens to live on this planet in the future will flinch and hide at the word *Braxian*! Ride with glory! Fight with honor! Protect our people!"

His arm comes down, and the warriors roar, the sound almost deafening as they stream out of the camp entrance, galloping toward the battlefield.

I glance at Nevada, who is staring at the other side of the camp, where Rakiz is about to leave with his warriors. The air between them suddenly seems electric as they hold each other's gaze, and then she finally grins, blowing him a kiss, and he nods, saluting her with his sword.

"That man," she says. "Can you believe he's making me stay in here?" She suddenly looks so disgusted that I almost laugh.

"To be honest, I'm surprised you let him bench you."

Nevada scans our surroundings and then leans close, her voice lowering. "I'd be out there with him, but I just found out I'm pregnant. Would you believe that? These warriors have some kind of super sperm, so you may need to be careful unless you want to be planning playdates with Ellie and me."

My mouth drops open. "Wow, um...are you happy about it?"

"Oh yeah, I am. I mean I'm a little pissed at the timing, but at least I'm not puking at everything in sight like Ellie. It's just...hard staying behind. If Rakiz dies and leaves me as a single mother to his giant warrior baby, I'll kill him."

I can't help but laugh as I finger the birth control implant in my upper arm. No giant alien warrior baby for me.

The sound of the battle swells, swords clashing, the roars and screams overwhelming to the ear. It's everywhere, the battle so close that it feels as if the warriors are just a few feet away.

We head back toward the healers' kradi, but instead of going inside, Nevada glances back at me, and we skirt around it.

"Come this way," she murmurs, and I raise my eyebrows as she heads toward a rarely used area within the camp that's tucked away behind the main cooking kradi.

"Check this out," she says, and I grin as I take in the crates that she's hidden behind a large piece of wood. We stack the crates up and climb to the top until we can finally see above the camp and across to the battlefield.

Most of our forces are in place, and we stand in tense silence as the Braxians charge into the fray. The Voildi have sheer numbers, and Killis has obviously managed to convince them to die for the cause as they attack with zero strategy except to overwhelm the warriors.

Unfortunately, that strategy seems to be working.

Terror makes my hands shake as my eyes find Zarix's large form on the front lines. He roars, taking down Voildi after Voildi, but it seems as if their numbers never decrease. There are always more waiting to attack.

"What happens when they get tired?" I murmur, and Nevada glances at me.

"This will be over before those hard-headed males get tired. Have you seen them train?"

Her voice is light, but I can hear the slight tremor in it, and she leans against me for support as Rakiz and his warriors attack the Voildi from the south.

"I need some damn binoculars," I say.

We took out a good chunk of the Voildi army with our exploding pods and crossbows. But who knows if it'll be enough to make a difference?

"There's Killis," Nevada spits, and I squint in the direction she's pointing. The bastard is riding another mishua, who has also been mutilated. I grind my teeth. The mishua are proud, intelligent creatures. I have no doubt that the poor thing understands exactly what she's being forced to do.

Nevada is right. Killis is wearing an eye patch. *Nice work, Ivy.*

Lafa's tribe marches behind most of the Voildi, and it's evident that Killis is using his own people as nothing more than meat for the Braxians' swords in an effort to exhaust them and slow them down. Then the traitors will swoop in, and the worst of the war will begin.

"I can't handle watching that man fight without me," Nevada mutters, her face pale. "Distract me or something, will you? What's going on with you and Zarix?"

I sigh. "We're kind of all over the place. He just told me he loves me. And I love him too. But is it enough?"

Nevada raises an eyebrow. "You think you'll stay and find out? Or will you go back to Earth?"

I open my mouth, and she elbows me in the ribs. "Take Zarix out of the picture. Could you be happy on Agron?"

"I don't know. I have a career I love on Earth. But at this point, I don't even know if I could keep dancing. I had only just recovered from an injury that almost kicked me into retirement, and now I've disappeared right before opening night. Other than dance, I have nothing on Earth. My parents are dead. I've got no degree and barely any savings. I don't even have any friends who aren't dancers themselves. No matter what I choose, it's likely that I'm going to be starting my life from scratch."

Nevada nods. "And what if you take Zarix into consideration? The question you need to ask yourself is if you'd be willing to give up everything and stay on this planet for him.

If that answer is no, it's best to just break it off quick. Like ripping off a Band-Aid."

The idea hurts. It hurts enough that my hand reaches up to rub at my tight chest. Nevada doesn't miss the movement and tilts her head.

"You don't have to make a decision now, you know. When Alexis made that deal with Dexar, he agreed that if his warriors found any human women, they'd return them to Rakiz's tribe. You're more than welcome to come back with us."

I think about her words for long moments while we watch the battle. Loving Zarix is hard, and I don't know if he'll ever be in a place where he feels he can risk truly being with me. Right now, we've spent almost every moment together since we met. But the fact is Zarix doesn't *want* to love me.

I frown as I squint into the distance. "Does the tide seem to be turning?" I ask. "Or is it just wishful thinking?"

Nevada studies the battlefield as her hand slides down to caress her sword. She opens her mouth, but my attention is elsewhere as I tense, cursing.

"What?" Nevada asks.

"Javir, that little shit. He slipped his guard. Oh my God, he's going to get killed."

I leap off the crates, determined to do something—anything. All I know is that the kid's going to die, and I can't handle the thought of this world without Javir's fast hands and gap-toothed smile.

I'm suddenly choking, and I claw at the arm that's fastened around my throat, my nails scratching desperately.

"Freeze or die," a voice rumbles, and I freeze.

The warrior holding me turns, allowing a tiny amount of air to slip down my throat. Nevada is crouched on the crates, crouching, her sword in her hand. She snarls at the warrior facing her, and he laughs.

I've seen him before. I have no idea what his name is, but he's one of Tecar's warriors. This is the worst kind of betrayal.

"You think you can take me, big boy?" Nevada taunts, tilting her head as she considers him.

He growls. "I'll kill you for daring to think a female can carry a sword."

Nevada grins savagely, her thighs tensing as she poises to leap and fight.

"Stop," the warrior holding me says, once again cutting off my air until I claw at his huge arm.

I know that voice.

Something sharp digs into my side, and I go so still I barely breathe.

"Put down your sword, female, or your friend dies."

Nevada stares at me, and I attempt to communicate with my eyes.

Don't do it. They'll just kill both of us.

She slowly lays down her sword, her lips bloodless as she shakes with rage.

"Get down," the voice behind me orders, and I watch helplessly as Nevada jumps off the crates. I tense as the warrior slides his knife or sword up my side, and cool air hits my skin as it cuts through my dress.

He relaxes his arm enough for me to gasp out a few words.

"Zarix will kill you for this, Perik."

CHAPTER SEVENTEEN

Z arix

I roar, killing Voildi after Voildi. Their numbers are strong, but I have little doubt that after this battle, they will no longer outnumber Braxians by such a huge margin.

I look forward to it.

My face is wet with blood, continually spraying from the creatures who attack with barely a thought. They hope to overwhelm us, assuming that their sheer numbers can make up for what they lack in size, speed, and training.

Braxian warriors train for battle from the moment they can walk. Voildi hunt in packs—not because they want to but because they have to.

Killis will be responsible for the almost complete eradication of his race.

Lafa sits on his mishua in the distance, surrounded by Braxian and Voildi. His face is a mask of fury as Rakiz fights his way toward him, cutting through Voildi to the south.

Tecar drives his elbow into my side, and I turn, avoiding the sword that sails toward my face. A Braxian warrior. I search his face, looking for familiar features.

No. He's too young to be my father.

Our swords meet, and Tecar slides his sword into the warrior's side. The warrior growls, and Tecar kicks out, his powerful leg pushing the warrior off his mishua, leaving him to fall to the ground, where he's quickly crushed as the riderless mishua bolts with wild eyes.

"Distraction kills," Tecar says. "Attempt to find your father in this battle, and you won't return to your female."

He turns away as another of Lafa's warriors attack, and I grind my teeth as I cross swords with a huge male. Tecar is right. I block out the warrior's face as I swing my sword, and my kills begin to blur together until I'm wet with blood.

Lafa roars as Rakiz meets him in battle, and I force my attention away. The tribe king refused to fight from anywhere but the front lines, and to have suggested otherwise would have been an unforgivable insult. However, both Rakiz and Tecar are now targets as Killis and Lafa direct all their attention toward taking them down.

And then it happens. Some of the Voildi begin to retreat.

I laugh as hundreds of them break and flee. And so we are left with Lafa's tribe and the few hundred Voildi that Killis trusted to defend him.

One of Lafa's warriors swings his sword, aiming for my head. I block with my own sword, and he glances behind me, face turning purple at the sight of the Voildi falling over each other to leave the battlefield.

"Traitors!" he roars.

"What did you expect?" I growl.

This warrior is fast and desperate—a lethal combination. Lafa's warriors are fresh in comparison to those of us who fight with Tecar's tribe. Most of Lafa's warriors have been waiting astride their mishua while we cut down Voildi after Voildi.

Unlike me, this warrior is not covered in blood, and it requires every drop of my concentration to meet each swing of his sword.

"Son!" a voice roars, and I tense. My eyes stay on the warrior, but his sword slips through my defenses, the tip slashing across the side of my neck before he thrusts it at my chest.

His eyes widen as his sword slides off my armor, and I lash out, my sword knocking his out of his hand as I direct Rexi, lunging forward and burying my sword in his throat.

He collapses off his mishua, and I turn, staring my father in the face.

He's older, of course, and it's shocking to see the impact life has left on his body. He still looks fit and strong, and I attempt to bury hurt at his betrayal under fury.

"Do not dare call me such. I would rather have no father than one who is a traitor."

"You know nothing," he snaps, bringing his mishua closer.

"I know you fled our tribe and now fight against them. If Mother was alive, she would kill herself from the shame."

His hand is clenched around his sword, and I note the slight tremble in his arm.

"Your mother wasn't killed by an animal," he spits. His face is so flushed with fury, his expression so completely deranged, that he's almost unrecognizable.

"What are you talking about?"

"She was killed by sword. Someone in the tribe murdered her. When I took this information to Hariz, he told me I was grieving and mistaken. But I know what I saw."

I stare at him. Hariz is Dexar's father, now dead and buried. The tribe king was an honorable man who would never have covered up her murder. My father has somehow forgotten that I also saw my mother's body. She had been mauled, the claw marks unmistakable. Does he truly believe this? Or is it just a way to justify his betrayal?

"Her body was ripped apart by something with claws. Why would you claim otherwise?"

"Lies!" he snarls, and I clench my jaw. If he truly believes this, his mind has broken. Perhaps he needed someone to blame for his mate's death. Needed somewhere to vent his feelings of helplessness and rage.

My mother was a wise female. Gentle and kind. Unfortunately, she knew better than to go walking without any protection. Two mishua had already been attacked, and our sentries had warned the tribe about the threat of hungry beasts as the cold season dragged relentlessly on.

My mother was smart, but she made a mistake. A "bad call," as Beth would say. Just as Hana did. Both of them knew better than to leave the camp while unprotected.

The thought slams into me, squeezing my chest until it feels as if I will suffocate. All this time, I've felt as if the fault lay completely with me. From the look on my father's face, he felt the same. So he turned his attention elsewhere, choosing to believe he was betrayed by his tribe. And I? I turned my attention inward, believing that I didn't deserve to have love.

I wasn't lying. I *do* love Beth. I thought it didn't matter. That my love was irrelevant, given my past.

Instead, it's the *only* thing that matters.

"Join with me, son. Join with Lafa, and we will make Dexar pay for his father's arrogance."

Distantly, I'm aware that the battle is ending. Voildi have fled, and even some of Lafa's warriors are moving away, likely hoping to escape the punishment they're owed for betraying their people.

"You are wrong," I bite out. "Your mind has been twisted, and you can't even see what you have done. You could have stayed and been a father. Instead, you joined with the Voildi? I am shamed to be known as your son."

My father's face darkens to an even deeper purple, his knuckles turning white as he clutches his sword. Then he glances over my shoulder, and a slow smile spreads over his face.

"I believe I have something that will change your mind."

In the distance, Rakiz roars, and I spin, my blood running cold as Perik and Zetri drag Beth and Nevada onto the battlefield, close to the camp's entrance.

"You will die for this," I choke out, turning my mishua.

"Be careful how you threaten me, son. I currently have everything you hold dear."

Beth's face is white, while Nevada is flushed with rage. Both females are shaking, and Rakiz pounds past me on his mishua as he leaves Lafa for Tecar to kill.

My mishua draws even with Rakiz's as I select and discard possible options. He glances at me, and we automatically separate, approaching the females from opposite sides.

"Careful," Perik's voice sounds over the remaining battle. He shows me the long knife in his hand, the lethal blade positioned next to Beth's delicate skin.

I'm wearing her dragon scale. What little protection she had is covering my heart.

"Let them go or die," I snarl, and Perik grins at me.

"You don't seem to understand," he says. "You no longer tell *me* what to do. I now tell *you* what to do."

"Perik?" Tazo's voice is hoarse, and I meet his gaze. He's approaching from the south, while Rakiz has moved in from the north, and I urge my mishua forward from the east as Tazo distracts Perik and Zetri.

Zetri jerks his head, shaking Nevada. She looks like a child next to him, and Rakiz freezes as Zetri holds her by her neck. He has no weapon, but he does not need one. He could break her neck in an instant.

Tazo moves closer, his gaze desperate as it meets mine.

"What do you want?" Rakiz growls, and Zetri laughs.

"Take your sword and drive it into your heart. Then I'll let her live."

"No," Nevada says. "No, no, no, no, no!"

She twists in Zetri's arms, and he snarls, shaking her.

"Karja, it is done," Rakiz says, and Perik grins at me as I jump off my mishua.

My father's voice sounds from over my shoulder. "I want you to have everything you want, son. If you want this strange, alien female, you will have her. As long as you join with us."

Tazo is moving closer to Beth, and I turn to my father, hoping to distract him.

"If I join with you, you will free both females."

My father tilts his head, considering.

"No," a voice sounds, and we all turn. Somehow Killis is still alive. He sits on a mishua, likely driving the poor animal insane with his scent. He has removed her horns and tied her mouth shut, having positioned sharp pieces of wood along the underside of the saddle, which dig into the mishua's scales until blood runs down her sides.

"How the fuck did you guys not kill this asshole?" Nevada asks, and Zetri slaps her across the face. Rakiz steps forward, his entire body shaking with rage.

Behind them, Javir raises his head from where he's crouched near the camp walls, his face draining of color as he stares at Beth.

Across the battlefield, someone roars, and we all turn as Tecar slides his sword into Lafa's gut. But I have no room for satisfaction as the traitor falls to the ground.

Tecar jumps from his mishua and ends Lafa's suffering, his eyes hard as he lifts his head and takes in our current situation.

Killis growls as Tecar mounts his mishua and makes his way toward us, sword swinging out as he casually beheads a fleeing Voildi.

"We offered to spare the females and children, and you declined," Killis says. He smiles at Nevada. "I told you I would take your eye."

She raises one eyebrow coolly, but her face pales as Zetri grabs her by the hair, ready to pull her toward Killis.

Beth screams, reaching for her friend, and I'm lunging toward her before I realize I have moved.

"Uh-uh," Perik says. He slices his knife up Beth's side, and I take a step forward, then freeze as he holds the knife close. "I will gut her in front of you, Zarix."

Never before have I felt this helpless.

I would take the slice of that knife a thousand times if it meant that Beth didn't have to, yet all I can do is watch and wait, hoping for my chance.

Beth will not be taken from me.

Javir pokes his head up from where he is now hiding behind one of the huge boulders that mark the camp's entrance. He meets my gaze, and I catch a flash of a blade before he ducks his head again.

He's showing me his weapon. I turn my attention back to where Beth is staring at me, tears running down her cheeks.

We speak two different languages, the communicators the only way we can understand each other. Yet I have memorized the shapes her lips make when she tells me she loves me.

She mouths the words now, tears in her eyes, and I step forward.

"Take me instead," I say.

"No," my father growls, but I pay him no attention.

Killis studies me and laughs. "Oh, how these proud warriors fall, so quick to beg. Your tribes will be no more thanks to a few weak alien females."

Javir chooses that moment to strike.

Beth

My side burns, but if these motherfuckers think they're going to kill us in front of our warriors, they're idiots. My heart aches at the expression on Zarix's face as he stares at me, shaking with fury.

That's his father near him. The huge warrior on the mishua. I can see similarities in the way that they look, and he called Zarix "son" earlier. Zarix's face completely shut down at the word, and he hasn't looked at his father again.

Perik twists slightly, and I manage to make eye contact with Nevada. Her eyes are clear and hard, and the look on her face helps me wrestle with the fear that's threatening to rise up and engulf me.

I blow out a long breath, and she gives me a tiny nod. We didn't end up on this planet just to die horrible deaths.

"I'm going to be sick," I murmur, and Perik automatically leans back slightly. Then the asshole holding Nevada screams, and I break out in a cold sweat as I see Javir's blue face, his jaw set in the stubborn expression I know all too well.

He moves like a flash, sliding his knife along the back of Nevada's attacker's knees, and he passes her the knife as the warrior folds. Perik jolts forward, waving his knife at Nevada, who he's obviously deemed the biggest threat.

I slam my head back into his face so hard that I see stars. Then I twist, snapping my leg up in a grand battement. This time, however, the move isn't pretty, and I bend my knee, jerking my head out of the way as I slam my foot into his chin.

I fall, off balance, but the warriors are there, and within moments blood sprays my face as Rakiz and Zarix kill the traitors.

I sit in shock, my hands shaking, and I watch as if from a distance as Killis attempts to turn his mishua, his eyes wild.

The mishua seizes her moment, not giving in to his awful torture as he digs the sharpened wood into her side. She swings her head from side to side, refusing to move, but she lets out a groan as Killis digs the wood into her. Enraged, Killis stands in his saddle, leaning forward to hit the mishua in the face, and the mishua takes her chance. With a roll of her shoulder, she flips the Voildi off her back.

She stomps forward as Killis crawls backward on his hands, the terror on his face obvious. With a low growl, the mishua kicks Killis in the head, killing him in the blink of an eye. It's so fast it's almost anticlimactic.

The mishua snorts, blood running down her side, and

the sight of her is so sad that I let out a shaky sob, tears dripping down my cheeks.

And then Zarix is there, hushing me as he pulls me into his arms, rocking me like a baby. He's holding me so tight he's almost crushing me, but I don't care, crawling up his body until I can bury my face in his neck.

"I thought I'd lose you," he murmurs, stroking my hair as he clutches me to him. I shake and cry, sobbing against him.

"Is she okay?" a voice asks, and I pull back, wiping tears off my face.

I reach for Javir, who kneels and winds his arms around my neck. For a moment, all three of us are joined in a group hug.

"I'm fine, I promise," I say.

Zarix clears his throat. "You were very brave," he tells Javir, who turns a darker shade of blue as he flushes. "Your actions helped save Beth's life."

I narrow my eyes at Zarix.

"Still," I say to Javir, "that was dangerous. You won't do that again, agreed?"

Javir rolls his eyes, and the males share a look. I sigh.

"You need a healer," Zarix says to me. In front of us, Rakiz has his arms wrapped around Nevada, who sends me a thumbs-up. Rakiz's face is hard, and he glowers at the bodies of the traitors as if he wishes he could kill them again.

Zarix gets to his feet, holding me close, and I'm numb as we walk through camp. Injured warriors line up outside the healers' kradi, and I tense in his arms.

"They need healing more than I do," I say, and he frowns down at me. "I am taking you to Rakiz's healer. I nearly lost you today. Please do not argue. I need to know for sure that you're okay."

I sigh but nod, and Zarix walks past the main healers' kradi and into another large, spacious kradi. There are a few warriors being seen to, but an old woman smiles at me as Zarix places me on an empty bed.

"My name is Moni, child. Now let me see where you're hurt."

I introduce myself and show her my wound, and she tuts, reaching for a tray of instruments. I grab Zarix's hand, and he kneels beside me, pressing kisses to my forehead, my cheeks, my mouth.

"Close your eyes," he whispers, and I comply, blowing out a breath as my side burns.

Moni is quick, and within a few minutes, Zarix is lifting me into his arms and striding back toward our kradi.

Someone has arranged for a large barrel of water to be brought in, and Zarix gently undresses me before wetting a large cloth and wiping every inch of my skin. He dries me tenderly, occasionally stopping to feather kisses along my shoulder or nuzzle my neck. At one point, he falls to his knees, and my mouth drops open as he wraps his arms around my stomach, careful not to brush the cut along my side.

He holds me close, and his huge body shudders for a long moment. His voice is hoarse, and my eyes fill with tears again as he trembles, obviously fighting not to fall apart. "Never again, Beth. Never. Promise me."

"Shh. Never again," I murmur. "I promise."

He nods and gets to his feet, his face paler than I've ever seen it. Then he helps me lie down on our furs and strips, cleaning the blood off his body, his movements matter-of-fact.

He leans over me. "I want you to rest," he says. "I need to meet with Tecar and Rakiz, but I will be back as soon as I can."

My voice is small. "Will you stay with me until I fall asleep?"

"Of course." He lies down beside me, wraps his arm around me, and strokes my hair soothingly until my lids grow heavy.

Beth

I blink open my eyes as someone strokes my face.

Zarix.

I pull him close as it all comes back to me. We're all safe.

"Were there many lives lost?" My voice is hoarse, and I wonder how long I slept.

"Fewer than two hundred warriors."

I reach up and stroke Zarix's frown away. "I'm sorry."

He nods, gently rolling until I'm beneath him, completely surrounded by his huge body. He leans over me. "We need to talk."

I raise my eyebrows. "Isn't that my line?"

"I have hunted for Dexar for many years, never spending the credits I was paid. My kradi is large, and I am entitled to rooms in Dexar's kradi if I want them."

I frown in confusion. I'm not quite sure why he's telling me this, but his eyes are intent, so I simply nod.

"There are other warriors here. Warriors that are not as...difficult as me. Warriors that are good at talking, with easy smiles. Warriors that deserve a female like you. But I'm begging you to be with me. Come back to camp and be my mate, Beth. No warrior could love you better than I could."

I open my mouth, but the words don't come out. I'm suddenly speechless. Zarix obviously takes my silence as denial, and his eyes widen slightly, his voice rough.

"I know I pushed you away. I was determined not to risk loving someone ever again. But you made me love you, and now I can't do anything else. I know I don't compare to your dancing, but I swear, if you let me love you, I will spend the rest of my days determined to make you feel the same way about me."

And just like that, I know my life will never be the same. Dancing was everything until a hard-headed warrior saved my life and made me want things I never wanted before. My career was always going to end at some point, but Zarix? When he loves, he loves fiercely. His love is forever, which is why he refused to let anyone close.

A tear spills down my cheek, and Zarix brushes it away.

I let out a choked sob.

"Of course I want to be with you. I love you, Zarix."

Pure relief crosses his face, and he leans down, taking my mouth.

"Ew," a voice says, and my hands come up, pushing against Zarix's hard chest as we both turn our heads.

Javir gives us both an impatient look. "Does this mean I need to find a new kradi?"

I burst out laughing, and both males stare at me, identical expressions of confusion on their faces.

EPILOGUE

B eth

"Close your eyes," Zarix murmurs.

I tilt my head, holding back a grin. "You know, you don't have to keep arranging for all these surprises. I'm not going to suddenly change my mind. I chose your grumpy ass, remember?"

Zarix grins back at me, and I can't help it; I pull him close. Just a few months ago, I thought I'd never get to see his smile. Now he's smiling and laughing so much that his fellow warriors stare at him as if he's been possessed.

Javir sighs beside me. "Are you two going to be gross again?"

I shoot him a look. "We're being romantic," I say, and Zarix narrows his eyes at him.

"Find somewhere else to be," he advises, and Javir rolls his eyes but throws us a grin over his shoulder as he stalks out.

We're hanging in Zarix's kradi, which is indeed very large. It turns out that the kradi we stayed in last time we were here was a temporary one reserved for warriors who were away hunting. This whole time, Zarix has had a massive kradi just begging to be furnished, but he never spent enough time at camp to care about it.

Zarix is planning to surprise Javir with his own kradi next to ours, although he'll still join us for most of our meals. His mom was fine, but when we finally managed to get a message to her, she asked if we would mind keeping Javir with us while she gets back on her feet. Apparently Zarix has arranged for her hut to be rebuilt whenever she's ready, but for now she can't face going back to the place where her husband was kidnapped and her home was burned to the ground.

So for now, Javir's ours. And despite his quick fingers and bad attitude, neither of us would have it any other way.

"Close them," Zarix says, and then I'm grinning as he ties a piece of material around my eyes. He lifts me into his arms, and I strain my hearing, attempting to figure out where he's taking me.

He's no dummy. He's obviously instructed everyone to be quiet, and I pout, jolting as Zarix's warm lips find mine.

"Patience," he says.

He walks for a few more minutes and then pauses. He walks a little more and then pauses again. This happens a few more times until I'm practically vibrating with impatience.

Finally he places me on my feet. He takes a deep breath, and I smile. My warrior is nervous.

He removes the blindfold, and I gasp.

It's a dance studio.

Even wood planks line the floor, and from the jeweled-colored cloth on the walls, I'm guessing we're in Dexar's massive kradi.

Alexis or Nevada must have told him what I'd need. A large mirror stands on one side of the room, and Zarix has even set up a barre, made out of several pieces of thin, polished wood.

"Oh my God," I breathe.

He knew how much I missed dancing, and he somehow managed to construct this room for me without letting me suspect a thing.

"Will you show me your dancing?" He moves to the wall, where several low seats sit, and I almost blush at the heat in his eyes.

"Now?"

A single sharp nod.

"Let me warm up a bit first."

I go through my stretches, enjoying the feel of my body moving in a way it hasn't for a while. What will it be like to dance solely for the enjoyment of it? Not because I'm training, not because I'm performing, but just because I want to dance right now, in this moment. Because I want to share one of the best parts of me with the man who shares all of himself with me.

Zarix's gaze is warm as I bend and flex along the barre. He suddenly gets to his feet, his gaze on mine.

"I'll return in a moment," he says, and I nod, checking my form in the mirror.

Compared to the woman who danced for hours each day, I'm out of shape. But tears fill my eyes as I stretch, running through my warm-up.

Since the moment I was abducted, I spent my time wondering if it was all worthless. If all the sacrifices I made for ballet were for nothing. But it wasn't worthless. Nothing ever is. Sure, I'll never again step onto a stage. I'll never dance in a hand-sewn costume and bask in the applause. Never again will I dance until my feet bleed. But that doesn't mean it wasn't worthwhile. Ballet made me into the woman I am today. The woman with embarrassing feet, excellent posture, and a turned-out walk. It made me learn to fight for what I want, to never give up, and to enjoy the shit out of the good times.

It gave me the grit to survive an alien abduction. The strength and flexibility to kick Perik in the head. And the ability to do battle with my stubborn alien warrior.

Zarix is back a few minutes later, and I raise my eyebrows as I take in the woman with him.

She looks like she could be related to Javir, with the same blue skin and sharp teeth. She beams at me as she holds up an instrument similar to a violin.

Music. *Wow.* My cheeks feel hot as I glance at Zarix. He simply takes his seat, his huge legs stretched out as he raises his eyebrow as if saying, *Show me what you got.*

I laugh as the woman starts to play.

Because there's no pressure, just the fun and enjoyment of the moment, I see what I can do. I push off my left leg into a piqué manège, twirling across the floor and laughing as I catch Zarix's mouth dropping open.

I get lost in the music, the feel of my muscles stretching, the look of shock on Zarix's face. I twist into a few fouettés, lifting my arms and spinning again and again.

"Leave," Zarix grinds out, and I turn to see the woman shoot me a wink as she hauls ass out the door.

And then I'm in his arms, laughing as he pulls me close, his hands running over my body with desperate fervor.

My hands are just as desperate.

I clutch him close and then push him away, pulling the

clothes off his body. He rips off his shirt impatiently, and then he reaches for his knife.

I raise one eyebrow, and then I'm laughing again as he slices down the middle of my dress, which falls apart.

"I liked this dress." It was the only one short enough for me to dance in.

"I'll get you another one."

His eyes run over my body as he bares more skin to his gaze. When I'm naked, he steps back.

"Dance for me," he orders, his voice hoarse.

I feel my face heat, and I almost refuse. But his expression is so desperate, so *needy*, that I step back.

Never could I have imagined dancing nude. But something about Zarix makes me feel so sexually confident, so... free. I hesitate and then finally shrug my shoulders, sending him a saucy wink.

I bend into a plié as he moves further away, giving me some room. I move onto tiptoe and then throw him a grin. If he likes what he's seen so far, he's really going to go nuts for this. I'm feeling good. Warm and strong. So I leap across the room in a grand jeté, catching Zarix's lips parting as my legs spread high in the air.

Then I lean into an arabesque, my back leg coming up high off the ground as I raise my arms.

Zarix is suddenly there, his mouth crashing down on mine, swallowing my gasp. I run my hands down his body, ridiculously pleased to find him already naked. He pulls me even closer, and I trip him, laughing as I fall down to the ground with him.

There's nothing like the feel of him beneath me. Hard, and hot, and all *mine.*

I press my lips against his skin, running them over the blue-green of his shoulder and chest and moving lower as I explore his abs. A rough curse from above my head tells me that Zarix is appreciating my exploration.

I make my way down to the *V* of his lower abs, feeling his powerful thighs tensing beneath my body.

"You make me insane," he growls, and I laugh.

"You ain't seen nothing yet."

I take his hard shaft in my hand, stroking as he tenses further. I'm suddenly desperate to see my huge, powerful warrior lose control.

I take him in my mouth, and he immediately pushes my hair away from my face, his gaze meeting mine. His eyes are so bright that they almost look like they're glowing, and they're fixed on my face as if I hold the secrets to the universe.

I take him deeper, tearing a rough groan from his throat. He buries his hand in my hair, cursing as I reach down, cupping his heavy balls.

"Enough," he says, his voice strangled, and I simply laugh, angling my head so I can take him even deeper.

And then I'm suddenly in the air, blinking at him as he pulls me over him.

"No fair." I pout.

"Need you now."

His voice is low and rough, and he positions me against him, the heavy heat of him so close to where I need him.

I reach down and slip him inside me, gasping as he thrusts up, his hands splaying over my hips. Each time feels even better than the last with this man.

I ride him, moaning as he moves within me, filling me up. His hands move to my breasts, pulling and pinching at my nipples until I'm writhing against him. He leans up, replacing one of his hands with his mouth, and I snap my hips faster as I gulp for air.

His free hand slips down, finding the sensitive spot so close to where we're joined. I cry out as he strokes my clit, clenching around him. He moves his hands until they're back on my hips, and he's lifting me, helping me climb higher as I reach for the peak.

The pressure breaks apart, and my nails dig deep into his chest as I tremble, lost in ecstasy. He wraps his arms around my back, thrusting once more, and then finds his own release with a low growl.

We lie, out of breath, for a few minutes, and he strokes my back, the gentle play of his fingertips making my toes curl.

"Thank you for my studio. You didn't have to do this, you know," I murmur, suddenly sleepy.

"I want you to be happy here. With me."

"I am."

He moves his hand into my hair, gently stroking it back from my face, and I could almost purr.

"Watching you dance...there's nothing else like it," he rumbles. "You steal my breath."

I feel my cheeks flush. Even after a successful career as a dancer, being promoted to principal and dancing as Odette, the look in Zarix's eyes when he watches me...

Nothing compares.

"I was thinking," he says, and I lift my head, watching him as he contemplates the ceiling. "There are people in this tribe who would love to see you dance. Women and children who would love to learn."

I grin. "I could teach?"

He meets my gaze. "You can do whatever you like. As long as you stay here."

He looks suddenly lost for a moment, almost vulnerable. There's no guarantee that the others will even be able to get off this planet, although Nevada, Ellie, and I will help them as much as we can. And yet I occasionally catch Zarix looking at me with this exact expression. As if he's worried I'll change my mind.

I reach up and stroke a hand down his face. "I love you," I assure him. "I'll never leave you."

"Forever," he replies, pulling me close, and I smile as I feel him harden beneath me. "I'll love you forever."

THE END

I HOPE YOU ENJOYED SAVED BY THE ALIEN WARRIOR! IF YOU have a minute to leave a review, I appreciate them more than you can imagine.

WANT TO BE THE FIRST TO KNOW ABOUT FREEBIES, NEW releases and soon... audio? Sign up for my free newsletter here.

ALEXIS AND DEXAR'S STORY IS NEXT IN SEDUCED BY AN ALIEN Warrior, and sparks are flying in his kradi ;)

STAY SAFE AND HAPPY READING!

Hope x